# Muffins

# &

# Moonbeams

by Elizabeth Maddrey

Scripture quoted by permission. Quotations designated (NIV) are from THE HOLY BIBLE: NEW INTERNATIONAL VERSION®. NIV®. Copyright © 1973, 1978, 1984 by Biblica. All rights reserved worldwide.

Cover design ©Book Cover Bakery.
Cover art photo ©konradbak used by permission.

Published in the United States of America by Elizabeth Maddrey
www.ElizabethMaddrey.com

Publisher's Note: This novel is a work of fiction. Names, characters, places, and incidents are either products of the author's imagination or used fictitiously. All characters are fictional, and any similarity to people living or dead is purely coincidental.

## Other Books by Elizabeth Maddrey

Arcadia Valley Romance – Baxter Family Bakery Series

*Loaves & Wishes* (in *Romance Grows in Arcadia Valley)*

*Muffins & Moonbeams*

*Cookies & Candlelight* (September 2017)

*Donuts & Daydreams (*March 2018)


The 'Operation Romance' Series

*Operation Mistletoe*

*Operation Valentine*

*Operation Fireworks*

*Operation Back-to-School*


The 'Taste of Romance' Series

*A Splash of Substance*

*A Pinch of Promise*

*A Dash of Daring*

*A Handful of Hope*

*A Tidbit of Trust* (Summer 2017)


The 'Grant Us Grace' Series

*Joint Venture*

*Wisdom to Know*

Then Jesus declared, "I am the bread of life. Whoever comes to me will never go hungry, and whoever believes in me will never be thirsty."
John 16:35

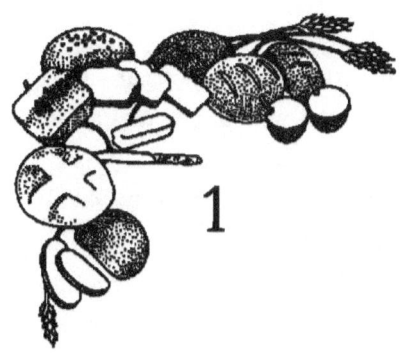

1

Malachi Baxter pushed a hand through his hair and scowled at the computer screen. He hadn't built a website since high school. How did he get stuck with this job? Oh, right. Business degree. Which meant handling the finances and such, but the website? He scooted away from the machine and stood. He needed to talk to his brothers.

He stepped out of the tiny office at the back of the bakery and into a wall of heat. His oldest brother, Jonah, was measuring ingredients into a huge mixing bowl. His lips were moving, but with his brother's face half-turned Malachi couldn't quite lip read well enough to make out the words. Was he singing? He touched Jonah's shoulder.

"Hey, Mal. Done with the website already?" Jonah set the measuring cup aside and dusted his hands on the apron tied around his waist. "That was fast."

Malachi shook his head and signed. "We need to hire someone. It's an investment that'll pay off in the long run. If I do it, it's going to look like someone's ten year old put it together over the weekend."

Jonah laughed. "That bad?"

Malachi nodded. He'd drag his brothers back to see what he'd been playing with all morning if they insisted, but it was embarrassing.

"All right. Let's check with Micah, but if you say we need it and can afford it, then I'm game." Jonah strode across the kitchen to the swinging door that led to the front of the bakery where Micah manned the counter.

Malachi sighed and followed.

Micah handed change and a bag of bread to one of their regulars—Malachi searched his memory for the name and came up blank—and turned when the light above the door that served as the hearing impaired version of a doorbell flashed and the customer left. "Uh oh. If Mal's out of the office, something must be up."

Malachi clutched his stomach and feigned laughter before sticking his tongue out.

Jonah shook his head. "Nothing serious. Mal thinks we should hire the website out."

"Rusty?" Micah raised his eyebrows.

Malachi signed, not bothering to speak along with it since they were alone in the bakery. "When was the last time you did a website?"

"Fair enough. Works for me. You notice I didn't volunteer to do any of that stuff, right?" Micah squatted and collected a towel from under the counter. He ran the cloth over the display case, scrubbing at some imagined spot. "Do what you think is best."

Jonah nodded. "Agreed. And since you're handling all the business end, I don't really care about details. You've got a good head on your shoulders and won't dig us into debt."

It was good his brothers had faith in him. Someone needed to. He nodded and eased back through the door into the kitchen. No point in hanging around out where customers came to gawk at the deaf man. In D.C. he hadn't been a novelty. There all sorts of people in the greater metropolitan area that made up what had been home his whole life. And mostly people didn't bother staring at the ones who were different. In Arcadia Valley different stuck out. Oh, they were nice about it. Malachi doubted anyone genuinely had any motive other than learning about something they didn't encounter every day. But that didn't keep him from feeling like a circus sideshow because he couldn't hear. He hadn't felt that way since right after the accident that cost him his hearing when he was young.

Back in the office, he pushed the door mostly shut, a signal that he was involved and shouldn't be disturbed if at all possible. A quick search online revealed what he suspected, there were more web designers in the world than made sense. How did he sort out the bad ones and find the good? Malachi drummed his fingers on the desk and reached for his cell phone to tap out a quick text to his sister, Ruth. The B&B had a nice site with a lot of the same kinds of functionality that they'd need. He set his cell back in the charging cradle that flashed brightly when his phone vibrated and turned to the computer. It was mid-morning. Ruth was probably cleaning rooms and wouldn't get to her phone for a while. But there was no rush.

With a glance toward the door and only the barest twinge of guilt, Malachi started up Orion's Quest and logged in. There weren't many players online in the middle of the morning, but there were always folks in other time zones, or people, like him, sneaking in a battle during a slow time at work. He skimmed the activity log. No one he played with was on, but he'd been storing up solo missions. Maybe he could knock one of them out. If his ship was repaired. He'd parked it in a dry dock when he logged out the night before, there should have been enough time for the fixes to be finished. And if not, he'd wander this outpost—where was he again? Didn't matter, really. Some new outpost on the edge of civilized space, getting ready to head into the frontier and see where his fortune lay. Before that, he could use an armor upgrade. Maybe some new weapons. If he had the cash after he paid for repairs.

The chat bar at the bottom of his screen notified him that Scarlet Fire had logged in. His heart sped up and he grinned as he opened up a direct message box.

"What are you doing on in the middle of the morning? Don't you have work?"

"Ha ha. I could ask you the same thing. Slow day?"

Malachi glanced at his cell phone cradle before typing again. "Waiting on a text. Thought I'd check on my ship, maybe start a quest."

"Need a first mate?"

Colorful lights flashed in the corner of his eye. Of course. He sighed and grabbed the phone. Sure enough, Ruth had come through with the contact info for her web designer. "Never mind. Gotta run. You'll be on tonight?"

"Of course. See you then."

Malachi took two minutes to run down and spring his ship from the repair facility. At least that way when he did have time to play he'd be ready to go. With a final check that he'd set himself to be able to scoot out on a mission as soon as he logged back in, he exited the game and opened a web browser. He liked the website for the Fairview, but there was nothing wrong with checking out other references just to be sure before making contact.

"You sure you won't come to church with us?" Ruth frowned as she signed.

He shook his head. Sunday morning was hard enough with everyone staring at Ruth signing during the sermon and special music. And then, out in the foyer, anyone who tried to talk to him either yelled, as if that was somehow going to help, or spoke slowly as if it was his brain that had been injured and not his ears. Both made it more challenging to read lips. He didn't need that on Wednesday night, too. "You don't have to babysit me. I'm okay."

"Don't you think if you were around them more it would help? The people at church are really nice, Mal."

"I believe you. I'm just...it's hard to be the weird new kid again. I thought that was behind me. In D.C., even if the people didn't know a deaf person personally they'd been exposed to enough differences that they could just treat me like a person without any adjective attached. I don't want to be 'the deaf guy.'" Mal threw his hands in the air when he finished signing and turned to head upstairs to the room he shared with his brothers at the B&B. And that was another thing they needed to address. Sharing a room with them temporarily was fine. But now that they were all settling here? Something had to give. And Ruth needed the space back, anyway. He'd seen her telling people she was booked up when, in reality, it was just her brothers taking up space.

Ruth touched his arm.

He turned, flinching inside at the sorrow written on her face.

"I'm sorry. You didn't have to move out here. If it's that bad...you don't have to stay." Her shoulders fell.

Was it possible to be a bigger jerk? He held out his arms and waited for her to walk into them. Since it was just Ruth, he could speak without worrying she was listening for the telltale signs of his deafness. "I'm glad to be here. If you're all here, then it's where I need to be. It's just...hard. And...I miss Mom and Dad."

Ruth leaned back and held his gaze, her eyes filling with tears. "I do too. Every day. I thought the years were supposed to make it easier."

He smiled and kissed her forehead before releasing her and tucking his hands in his pockets. With

Ruth it was never an issue to talk without signing. Even if he didn't know what he sounded like. Half the time he imagined it was still the voice he remembered from his childhood, but it had to have changed as he'd grown up. Maybe, if he was lucky, he sounded a little bit like Dad. At least in his mind, Dad's baritone had been warm. Friendly. "Do you need me to go tonight?"

"No. No, I don't need you there for me. I just think you might find something there for you."

He scoffed but didn't ask exactly what she had in mind. As a recently engaged woman, Ruth was probably scouting the single ladies with an eye toward her brothers. But he'd been in high school when he'd given up on the delusion that he'd ever marry. The few deaf girls he'd dated had wanted him to turn his back on his hearing friends. And the hearing girls had treated him like he was a project. No. He was better off imagining love with someone like Scarlet Fire online than trying to navigate the real thing.

Malachi clicked on the mission, double checked that he had all the required equipment on board, and opened the map. He chose the first star system he'd need to visit and set the ship in motion. It wasn't instantaneous transport, which made the game a little more fun. Things could go wrong en route. There were pirates for one, and the handful of people who were irked at him for beating them to prizes. Most of them got over it and remembered it was just a game. But there were others who needed a stiff dose of reality. He tried to steer clear.

"Started without me?" Scarlet Fire's chat message popped up.

"Just barely. You can still join if you want."

"Sounds good. I'll beam in?"

"Perfect." Malachi closed out of the armor customizing screen he'd been in and ran through the halls of his ship to the transportation hub. He verified that it was her and clicked to allow her to join the party. Her avatar materialized. He swallowed. It wasn't as if he didn't run into roughly the same avatar all the time—you could only customize your clothes and hair—but something about hers always made his heart stop. Which probably meant he needed to get a real life. "Welcome. We'll hit the first system in about two minutes. How was your day?"

"Got a new client. Always a good day. Even better, they're a referral from a previous client and they're local."

"Don't you do web design? Why does local matter?"

"Doesn't necessarily. But sometimes it helps if there are hiccups." Her avatar's hair color changed from bright red to blonde. "What do you think?"

"It's different."

"Is that good or bad? Was trying to go a little more real to life." The hair changed back. "Maybe that's not a good thing?"

She was a blonde. It didn't fit his mental image. Not surprising as he'd essentially un-animated her avatar and dressed her in normal clothes when he was forming it. But...blonde worked, too. "No, I liked it. It just took me by surprise."

"Don't you ever want people to know the real you?"

He shook his head and tapped the keys to dock the star ship at the port where they'd find the first leg of their mission. The best part of online multi-player games was having the chance to be who he really was without first waiting for people to get over the fact that he was deaf. "Not really."

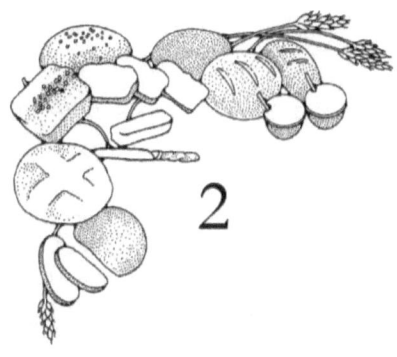

2

Ursula Franks rolled her head on her neck and pushed away from the computer. It was about time to grab some lunch, and then the afternoon stretched out in front of her with the promise of a brand new design instead of more maintenance. Not that there wasn't still maintenance work to do. There was *always* maintenance work to do. But she'd made a significant dent in the urgent items this morning, and starting on a new site was her reward.

Maybe she'd walk over and check out the bakery. It was only four blocks away and she could use the exercise. Ursula shook a couple of treats into her cat's bowl, smiling as the sound brought the grey striped tabby running. "There you go, Triton. I'm running out for a bit."

She slipped the strap of her purse over her neck so it hung diagonally across her body. That way she wouldn't have to keep fussing with it when she walked. After checking that she had her keys, she skipped down the front steps wincing as the midday heat rammed into her. The sun was bright. Ursula dug for her shades and pushed them on. Better. With a wave to old Mr. Greenway, who sat out on his porch in a lawn chair that was probably new when her parents were born, she aimed toward downtown and the Arcadia Valley Shopping Center.

It sounded grander than it was. The strip mall had been refurbished when Main Street was revitalized. But it was still a strip mall. Still, they were attracting good businesses, and that saved her from making trips into Twin Falls as often. Since she was out, she'd pop over to Benita's and get a couple of things she was running low on. In fact, maybe she'd grab a loaf of bread, snag a block of cheese next door, and head to the park to eat. It would add another mile to her trip but she could spare the time.

She tugged open the bakery door and breathed deeply as the yeasty scent of fresh bread surrounded her. Maybe she'd just sit at one of the two tables by the window and eat here.

"Can I help you?" The man behind the counter set aside the book he'd been reading—a recent sci fi novel that was on her list as well—and stood.

Ursula's breath caught in her lungs. No baker should look that good. Shouldn't bakers be chubby and grandfatherly rather than broad-shouldered hunks with just the right amount of scruff on their chin to make a woman's mouth water?

"Are you okay?"

"Yeah. Great. Hi. Sorry." Heat flooded her face as Ursula stepped closer to the counter. "My mind wanders."

The corners of his mouth poked up. "I have that problem sometimes too. First time here?"

She nodded and scanned the display case. They definitely leaned toward bread—which was what the man who'd emailed told her—but *bakery* conjured images of donuts and cookies and cakes. None of which were in evidence. "I'm Ursula Franks. You just hired me to do your website?"

"Sure. Hi. I'm Malachi. We emailed briefly yesterday." He leaned his arms on the case. "What can I get you?"

"Maybe a loaf of the asiago?"

His smile did crazy things to her belly. "Sure thing. That's one of our best sellers."

As he turned to get a bag and tongs, Ursula scanned the other offerings in the case. "You make all of this on site? By yourself?"

Malachi turned back, reached into the case, and slipped the bread into a bag. "Anything else?"

Her eyebrows lifted. Rude or...? "You made this?"

"Me?" He laughed, shaking his head. "No. My brothers are the bakers. I do the books and the dishes. You want to talk to them? They ran out to help my sister, but they should be back soon."

She considered. It might be nice to meet the actual bakers, get a feel for them and the business. But like she'd told MalRen last night online, she didn't need that face-to-face connection in order to do a good job on a website. That said...she wouldn't necessarily mind getting to know this brother a little. Even if nothing could come from it. "Tell you what. Would you mind if I ran down to Benita's and got some cheese and brought it back? I was going to make a lunch out of it at the park, but I could hang out and wait if you'd join me?"

He gave a little shrug. "Sure. I can slice this for you."

"Nah. I'll just rip off chunks." He made a valiant effort to control the wince, but she still saw it. Ah well. She handed him a ten, took her change, and glanced at the table in the corner, then back to him. "Okay if I leave it here?"

He nodded.

"Be right back." Ursula tossed the bread onto the table and pushed through the door back into the heat, away from the tantalizing aroma of bread. Benita's was just two shops down. A completely different mixture of smells—spices and vegetables, mostly—met her inside. The tiny refrigerated space had a decent selection of fancy cheese and, after a quick eenie meenie miney moe, she selected sharp white cheddar from Ireland. Since the Italian soda was right there at the checkout, she grabbed two bottles of the lemon flavor and added them to her order. If she was going to have a picnic, she might as well do it right.

Malachi looked up from behind the counter when she came back to the bakery. She lifted the cheese and sodas. "Hope you like cheddar."

"Can I get you a knife for the cheese?"

She laughed. "Fine. Yes, a knife would be grand."

He flashed a smile and came out from behind the counter. The broad shoulders hadn't been a lie. The man clearly worked out. Or he was genetically gifted. Or she needed to get out more. Her mother, certainly, would opt for the latter. "My brothers texted. They're on the way back."

Ursula sat in one of the wrought iron chairs and sniffed the bread before tearing off a hunk. She pushed one of the Italian sodas across the table. "That's for you."

"You didn't..."

"I know. But I did. Unless you don't like lemon?"

He twisted the cap and took a sip, his eyes lighting up. "This is good."

"So's this." She tapped the bread. "I see why you need a website. People need to know you're here."

Bells on the door jangled and a bright light flashed behind the counter as two men and a woman entered the bakery. The men bore a striking resemblance to Malachi, which meant genetically gifted was definitely the answer to her previous question. He stood and gestured for them to come over. "Ursula, these are my brothers, Jonah and Micah, my sister Ruth. She runs the Fairview B&B."

Ursula held up a finger and chewed fast, swallowing the lump of bread before she should have. She took a fast swig of soda and stood, wiping her hand on her shorts. "Sorry about that. It's so nice to meet you."

"I saw you fixed that issue with the calendar for the B&B this morning. Thanks. It was making me a little crazy." Ruth grinned and pulled a chair over from the second small table. "Is that the asiago? It's one of my favorites."

"It is. It's amazing. Malachi says you two are the bakers?" Ursula glanced at Jonah and Micah, who nodded. Malachi eased away from the group, the soda in his hand. Their gazes locked and he lifted it in a salute before drifting through the door behind the counter. She frowned. Why would he just leave like that? Jonah was talking. She dragged her attention back to the man and listened as he went on about the benefits of using local wheat and community-supported bakeries in general. Some of it, at least, would work for copy on the site. The man had passion, she had to give him that.

Ursula sorted through the items in her character's backpack and checked the player log again. Where was MalRen? She'd logged on and set a notification for him as soon as she'd gotten home from lunch. She'd still managed to get a decent start on the bakery website and take care of a few more urgent issues for existing clients, but her mind hadn't been on the work. Instead, she'd been replaying the brief interaction with Malachi Baxter. He was good-looking but not much of a conversationalist. Except...it felt like he *could* be. Like he was holding back. And she'd know. She did the same thing.

Ruth had been friendly. Ursula yearned to reach out and see if they could develop a friendship. Except...she shook her head. There was no point. They might manage a friendship for a little while, but ultimately, if history was any indication, at some point she'd do something without realizing it and everything would explode, leaving her picking up the tattered pieces of her psyche for months. Better for all concerned to be polite and professional and leave it at that. She wasn't cut out to have friends.

She reached for her cell as it started to ring. "Hi, Mom."

"Happy Thursday."

Ursula chuckled. "I didn't realize Thursdays were something to celebrate."

"Every day you're alive is something to celebrate. You know that."

She fought the urge to roll her eyes. Mom would know. She always did. "So what are you celebrating today?"

"Other than the fact that I have an amazingly talented daughter who fills my heart with joy?"

Ursula scoffed. "I reword my question: what do you need me to do?"

"So cynical. I never have figured out where you got that. Must be your father. I didn't want anything other than to hear your voice and check in. I'm still not sure why you live in Idaho when there are perfectly good houses to never leave right here in South Carolina."

"You're a laugh riot, Mom. I went for a walk at lunch today to check out the bakery that hired me to do their website." Her stomach grumbled and she pushed back from the computer and padded into the kitchen to cut another slice off the rapidly diminishing loaf of bread. "You should come visit and we could walk over together."

"Now who's the comedian? You know I don't fly. And I'm certainly not breaking that rule simply to taste bread. It might shock you, seeing as how you've been gone for so long, but we do have bakeries here."

Ursula laughed. "It was worth a shot."

"You're just trying to get out of coming home for Thanksgiving."

"Mom. It's July. Can we not worry about November yet?"

"I'm just saying that if you're planning on coming, there's no harm in keeping an eye on the airfare. You never know what kind of deals there might be."

"I'll set up an alert, okay?" She made a mental note to do that, though trading in the cold temperatures and chance of snow in Idaho for South Carolina wasn't high on her list. The weather had been one of many reasons she'd packed up and headed to Arcadia Valley. Maybe it was a little farther afield than she'd planned—she loved her family—but when she'd added up all the pros and cons, this place had won. Hands down. Most days, she didn't even regret it. "How's Dad?"

"Oh, you know your father. He spends all of his time playing that stupid computer game you got him for Christmas last year and leaves me to fend for myself."

"It's not stupid. You might even enjoy it. You could be Dad's crew. He and I hook up for missions when we can, but the time difference makes it a challenge." That and the fact that, according to Dad, at least, Mom only let him play for two hours a day and never in the evening. Which pretty much meant there was no chance they'd be online at the same time unless Ursula made a point of setting work aside. Which she sometimes did.

"Please. Anyway, other than that, he's doing fine. We're planning a trip down to Charleston next week. He wants to stop at some little towns along the way and see if he can find a few of the graveyards that are supposed to be there. It'll be nice to add to our rubbings. Assuming they're still there."

"Remember to wear long pants. You don't want to get a ton of chiggers again."

"I know, I know. Honestly, one time I forget and I never live it down. I only told you so you'd know if we weren't home. If you decided to call."

Like she ever had a chance to call. Mom called so often, there was no point. All she had to do was wait five minutes. "Or I could call Dad's cell phone if I was worried."

"That too. So a bakery?"

Ursula smiled and carried her bread back to the office. "I thought you might be curious. It's run by three brothers. They're new to the area and their sister took over the Fairview B&B—you remember I told you when the previous owner, Naomi, passed away?"

Her mother sighed. "That was so sad. So young. And really your only friend out there. Have you given any more thought to trying out a church? I know you attend ours online, but it isn't the same thing."

She wasn't going to get into that discussion. Naomi had, almost, convinced her to give Grace Fellowship a try. Then she'd gotten sick and...it was probably better this way. The problem was, her mother could be persistent. Unless... "They're all quite handsome."

"Oh?" How could her mother convey so many questions in one word? It wasn't a skill Ursula had managed. Yet.

"I'm going to have to get some photos for the website. I'll send them to you when I do."

"And?"

"And nothing. They're handsome. But for all I know they're married and have ten kids each." Okay, none of them had been wearing wedding bands. Although Ruth had sported a gorgeous engagement ring on her finger.

Her mother huffed out a breath. "Honestly, Ursula. I don't know why you take such joy in tormenting me. Maybe I will come out, after all. And then I can see about marrying you off to one of the bakers. If you're not going to come home, the least you can do is give me grandchildren."

Who she'd only see a handful of times a year, when Ursula and Fictional Husband made the trek to South Carolina. But there was no point in saying that. Grandchildren was the bone her mother never put down easily. She made a non-committal grunt. "I should run, Mom. Love you. Thanks for calling."

Shaking her head, Ursula plugged in her cell and scooted closer to her computer. Still no MalRen. Where was he? She ran through their conversation last night and...nothing. There was nothing that should have scared him off. But if things went the way they usually did, somehow she had.

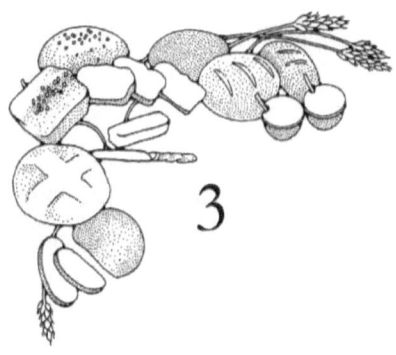

3

"I don't understand." Ruth signed as she spoke, her face the picture of annoyance. "What's wrong with the room upstairs?"

Malachi eyed his brothers. They were seated around the small table in the B&B's kitchen, along with Ruth's fiancé, Corban. Both arched their brows at him. Fine. He'd been the one to broach the subject at the bakery, sure, but they'd been in total agreement. Now, however, it appeared they were going to take the coward's way out. He signed, his throat too tight to speak. "There are three of us and we're all used to being on our own. It's...crowded."

Ruth visibly deflated. "Okay. I can see that. I'd offer you my rooms but it wouldn't solve the problem, just delay it for a bit."

Corban cleared his throat and finger spelled while he spoke. "I might have a solution."

Malachi cringed. It was great that the guy wanted to learn to sign. Flattering, even, that he cared enough about his sister to do it. But he needed a better book than whatever he was using. Reading lips was a lot easier than trying to spell everything and make something coherent out of it. "What's that?"

A slow grin spread across Micah's face. "I think I might know what you're going to suggest and I'm for it."

Jonah elbowed Micah. "Let the man speak."

"What if you came and lived at the farmhouse? I've got the room." Corban pushed the empty plate, a remnant of the dinner they'd shared, toward the middle of the table. "Wouldn't mind the company either. And since you're early risers as well, it shouldn't be a problem."

Malachi frowned. His brothers were early risers. He did everything in his power to sleep 'til the reasonable hour of seven. Which is why he got stuck manning the counter in the later afternoon hours. Or whenever they decided they needed a break. And sure, meeting Ursula today had definitely been a perk, but he usually spent the whole time wondering when he was going to mess up and miss a question or an order. Still, having his own room would probably be enough. If the lights weren't going on, he wouldn't wake. It's not as if the noise would bother him.

"In fact, that might just solve another problem your sister and I've been discussing." Corban glanced over at Ruth and held out his hand. She slipped her fingers through his and smiled. "Once we're married, I know my mom ran the B&B from the farm house, but Ruth thinks—and I agree—that it's more convenient if we live here. But I didn't want to let the farmhouse go unoccupied. If you're living there...well, it'll be taken care of."

Ruth nodded, though her eyes were unhappy.

"What's wrong?" Malachi touched Ruth's arm.

"I like having you here." She shrugged. "But you're right. It's cramped up there and, all things being equal, I could use the extra room for guests."

Jonah nodded. "Sounds like a plan. When do you want us?"

"Whenever. That's for you four to work out." Corban scooted his chair away from the table and began collecting the dirty dishes.

"Ruth?" Micah angled his head to the side.

"Go. Tonight's fine. I'm a big girl." She blinked her eyes and stood, reaching for the last of the dishes.

Jonah and Micah's chairs toppled backward as they left the kitchen, talking about packing. Malachi rose more slowly, watching his sister. She set the dishes in the sink and stood for a moment. He eased to the doorway, still watching. Ruth sniffled. Corban drew her into his arms. His gaze met Malachi's and one corner of his mouth lifted.

"She'll be okay."

Malachi didn't know if Corban spoke the words aloud or just mouthed them, but he nodded. She would. But he hadn't intended to hurt her.

Malachi edged toward the church doors and wished yet again that he'd driven himself instead of riding along with his brothers. Corban had fetched Ruth—and thankfully they'd escaped all going together by virtue of the car being too small. It made sense. Why drive three cars to go to the same place? But Jonah and Micah always ended up socializing after the service. It's what you did when you moved to a new place. Malachi got that. He just didn't happen to enjoy it. And, great, here came Mrs. Poncetta. Last week she'd cornered him to tell him all about the singles class. Like he hadn't already visited twice. What would it be this week?

Out of the corner of his eye, he caught a flash of blonde hair and turned. Was that...? Malachi turned and ducked out the door. He jogged across the parking lot as the woman walked, head down, toward the street. Slightly out of breath, he plucked at her sleeve.

Ursula stopped and turned, clutching her Bible to her chest.

Malachi grinned. "Ursula, right?"

She nodded, her lips curving into a tight smile. "Mr. Baxter. Hi. Did you need something? I don't actually work on Sundays..."

He arched a brow. Mr. Baxter? Why had he even bothered to chase after her? Sure, she was pretty, and she'd seemed friendly, but she was no Scarlet Fire. Which was exactly the problem. *No one* was Scarlet Fire. At least no one he knew. So...he should try to make friends offline. Or at least look like he was trying so his brothers would get off his back. And maybe stop teasing him about his online girlfriend. Scarlet Fire wasn't his girlfriend. Sure, maybe he'd basically decided she was the perfect woman—not that she was perfect. She had faults. She was always rushing into battle before he could come up with a plan. And she seemed to enjoy gossiping about other players—particularly if they did something stupid. But still, she was perfect for him. If he was ever going to fall in love, it'd be with her. At least with his own room, no one could complain if he stayed up later completing a mission. "No. Sorry, I just wanted to say hi. I haven't seen you at Grace before."

"Ah. No. First time."

"And?"

She shrugged. "It was okay. Not really any different from my usual."

It was like pulling teeth. "Which is where?"

Her lips thinned as she pressed them together. "Online. My parents' church, the one I grew up in, streams their services."

"So you're not from here, either?"

Ursula shook her head. "No. I grew up in South Carolina. I've been here almost five years."

He grinned. A tiny shred of common ground. "I almost went to college in Carolina."

"Me too." She turned to go.

Malachi chuckled. She was a tough nut. Though she didn't seem to be bothered by his voice. She knew he was deaf, didn't she? Seemed like everyone in town did—at least if the number of times he was greeted with, "Oh, you're the deaf one, right?" was any indication. So surely she did, too. Though in one corner of his mind he questioned the words, they still came out. "Want to grab lunch?"

Malachi clicked on the star map and chose his next destination. With a few more clicks, his ship was en route. Sunday afternoon stretched out ahead of him and, though he'd had offers from his siblings for various activities, he was better off in his room where, maybe, he could shake the gloom that had settled around his shoulders.

His chat box opened with a message from Scarlet Fire. "Whatcha' doin'?"

Malachi dragged the keyboard onto his lap and typed back. "Started the Zerillanskan mission. New bounties posted so I figured why not. You?"

"Hanging out to see if my Dad has time to play this afternoon. He needed help on the Ashkoars run."

That was a tricky one if you were on your own. "I still think it's fun that your dad plays."

"Convince my mom. She's always managing to slip in a little dig. He doesn't get online as much anymore. But it's fun when he can. Do anything fun this morning?"

Malachi sighed, Ursula's face as she turned down his lunch offer flashing to the front of his mind. "Fun? No. Church was good, then I made a fool of myself."

"What happened?"

"Asked someone out. Got turned down in no uncertain terms. Good times. At least it reminded me why I don't bother anymore. Not sure what came over me."

"Must be the day for it. I got asked out by a guy after church."

"Take it you said no?"

"Don't know him. He's good looking but..."

Malachi frowned. "Maybe you can help out the clueless male. How do you get to know someone if you don't do something with them?"

The cursor mocked him, blinking at him while she made no reply. It was a reasonable question, wasn't it? It wasn't like he'd asked Ursula on an actual date. Just lunch. After church. Despite the fact that reading lips during a meal could be tricky. He'd been willing to take the chance to try and make a friend. Whatever. Lesson learned.

His ship arrived at the programmed destination and he selected the computer players he wanted to accompany him. Frowning, he closed the chat box and set it to mute. Chatting during a mission was the best way to miss an objective. He did enough of that in real life.

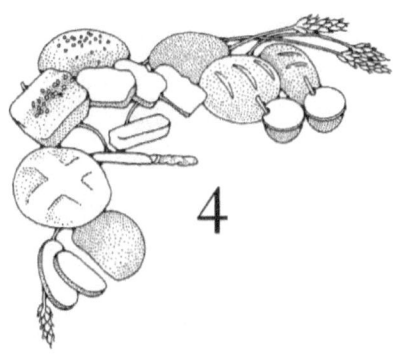

4

MalRen's question haunted Ursula into her Tuesday morning client calls. She'd logged off after he asked and missed out on meeting up with her dad, which, of course, sparked an email from him making sure everything was okay. And then there was a long phone call from Mom that was probably motivated by the same concern but had left her with a headache. She'd spent most of Monday working on the bakery website and thinking about Malachi. The website was coming together. Her thoughts about him...were not.

With a sigh, Ursula stood and crossed to the window of the room she used as an office. Mr. Greenway was out on his porch, so at least she knew aliens hadn't invaded. Should she have said yes? Part of her wanted to call and ask her mom. But that conversation would inevitably take the wrong turn and Mom would start knitting baby blankets. No, that was unfair. She'd only *think* about the blankets. Her advice, however, would be to go apologize and ask him to lunch.

Her stomach rumbled. Lunch wasn't a bad idea. She had to eat. Presumably Malachi ate. She'd just walk over there and...no. What was she thinking? He probably had no interest in her at all now. If there'd been anything other than friendly curiosity before. Which wasn't a guarantee. Men said women were complicated. They clearly had no clue about their own species. She could call her dad and ask...which would be worse than talking to Mom.

MalRen. He was a man. Well, okay, there was no actual guarantee there. Online you could be anything you wanted to be, but if he wasn't actually a guy then Ursula would give it all up and consider becoming a nun. Except for the whole becoming Catholic thing. Not that that was bad. She was just happy enough as a protestant. But she liked...procrastinating. Obviously.

Before she could talk herself out of it, Ursula was back in her chair and logged into Orion's Quest. There wasn't even a guarantee he'd be on. It was the middle of the workday. But she'd run into him enough times during the day, especially lately, that it was a distinct possibility. She scrolled through the player list and smiled when she spotted his name. With a quick prayer that this wasn't a huge miscalculation, Ursula typed out a chat message.

"Question for you—if I'm rethinking that whole Sunday lunch thing, do I go apologize and ask him to a meal, or will he take that the wrong way?" Ursula re-read the message and hit send.

Would he even answer? She'd disappeared abruptly on Sunday. She held her breath and let it out with a *whoosh* when he replied.

"Depends."

She winced. He was mad. And she didn't blame him. "I'm sorry I logged off on Sunday. Your question was valid and...that's why I'm trying to figure out how to fix things."

"Okay. Still depends."

Gah. Was he punishing her? Maybe he was multitasking. Benefit of the doubt. Better to give him that and play along. "Okay. On what?"

"What do you want? From him, I mean."

"To get to know him, I guess. You were right, okay? You can't get to know someone if you don't spend time with them." Not that she had high hopes that he'd still want to know her once they did that. But the pastor's sermon had been about letting go of past hurts. And maybe it was time to try to do that. Again. Even if it meant racking up a whole pile of new hurts.

"Then yes. That seems like a good, straightforward way to go."

Straightforward. Was she not supposed to be that way? It's who she was. She'd never been good at games. "Too blunt?"

"No. It's good. No games. Games are for the online world."

She chuckled. On that score, she and MalRen agreed. "Okay. Then...I guess I'm gonna take a walk. Mission tonight, maybe?"

"Sure."

Ursula frowned. Not a delighted reaction, but hadn't said no. Maybe she hadn't messed up this friendship yet after all. "See you then."

She logged out and grabbed her purse and keys. Should she drive in case he actually *was* free for lunch? They could probably still hit Sunrise Cafe. The Jukebox, if they missed it. And those were both far enough from the bakery that it was worth taking the car.

The bells above the door jingled. Ursula inhaled deeply. How could you work here and not eat everything that came out of the oven?

"Hi there. Ursula, right?" The man behind the counter smiled and set aside his cell phone. "What can I get you?"

"Hi. Micah, right?"

He grinned. "Got it in one."

"I was wondering if Malachi was in?" Ursula fought the urge to clear her throat and tucked her hands in the pockets of her shorts to keep from twisting her fingers together.

Micah's eyebrows shot up. "Sure. He's in the office. In the back. I'll take you through."

He gestured for her to come around the side of the display case and pushed open the door to the kitchen. The smell intensified as she stepped through. As did the heat. The other brother—Jonah? That sounded right. It was one of those Old Testament books anyway.—was up to his elbows in dough at a counter that ran the length of the space.

Micah pointed to the closed door at the back of the room. "Office is right there."

"Thanks." She managed a weak smile, along with a wave to Jonah, as she crossed the kitchen. Was she really doing this? She was. It was the right thing to do. She tapped on the door and listened. Nothing. Maybe he hadn't heard her knock.

"Just go in."

She jumped a little and turned.

Jonah smiled. "Seriously, it's okay."

"Okay." She breathed out the word and pushed open the door. "Malachi?"

Nothing. Ursula frowned. What was he...was that a computer game? She stepped more fully into the office and tapped his shoulder.

He jolted, minimized his screen, and pulled off his headphones as he swiveled his chair. He blinked, a slow smile spreading across his face. "Hi. Didn't expect to see you today. Is the website done?"

She shook her head. "No, not yet. Though I'm making some progress—I don't have it set up for outside access yet, but I can log you in and you can look at it if you want?"

Malachi shrugged. "That's okay. But...what brings you here?"

She took a deep breath. "I wanted to apologize. For Sunday. I...it probably doesn't matter why, but I'm sorry. And I wanted to see if the offer to get lunch together was still open?"

He studied her before nodding. "Sure."

"Are you free today? Have you eaten yet?"

He shook his head and rolled away from the computer. "I could eat."

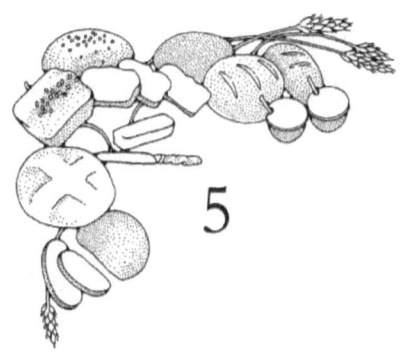

5

"You seem awfully chipper." Corban stomped his feet on the mat outside the kitchen door of the farm house before stepping inside. "You get a spreadsheet balanced or something?"

Malachi snorted and finished spreading mayonnaise on a piece of bread. Lunch with Ursula had been fun. And he suspected part of that was owed to her being Scarlet Fire. Unless he missed his guess. He flipped the bread onto the rest of the sandwich he was building and sliced it neatly in half.

"He had a hot lunch date." Jonah piped up from the kitchen table where he sat with a steaming bowl of soup.

"It wasn't a date." Malachi signed before picking up his plate to join his brother. He frowned at the soup. Who ate soup in July?

Corban pulled out a chair. "I missed that."

Jonah spooned up noodles and broth and blew across it. "He said it wasn't a date."

"It wasn't. It was lunch." Malachi spoke as he signed. Corban was practically family. And he *was* trying to learn to sign.

Corban smiled and grabbed an apple from the bowl in the middle of the table. "Who was your not-a-date with?"

"The web designer." Jonah smirked at his brother. "They're two peas in a pod. Both happier working with computers than people."

Malachi shook his head. Jonah had no idea. His brothers would tease him relentlessly if they ever found out Ursula was Scarlet Fire. The odds of meeting the one woman who was perfect for him in real life were astronomical. And okay, fine, he had a crush on her online persona. Tiny. Barely even a crush. Really more just a "Hey, she makes a great friend" vibe. And when his brothers first figured that out, it had been months before they'd let it go. Still came up occasionally if he made the mistake of talking about the game. There was no way he was cluing them in and starting it all up again—which they'd probably do in front of her.

"Wasn't she at church on Sunday?" Corban bit the apple and chewed. "Tall and blonde?"

Malachi nodded. He hadn't classified her as tall, but they were, roughly, eye to eye.

"Nice." Corban punched Malachi's arm.

"Thanks." Malachi signed. Corban ought to know that one. If he didn't, well, he wasn't trying.

"You're welcome." Corban spoke and signed, eyes sparkling. "See? I know a little. I'll get there."

Jonah blew across his soup again. "Not sure why you bother. He reads lips well enough I don't even sign at him all the time."

"Just seems polite, I guess." Corban lifted a shoulder and stood. "I'll let Ruth know you two won't be at dinner."

"I texted her." Malachi lifted his phone.

Jonah hunched his shoulders. "I was gonna let her know."

"Like I said, polite." Corban's shoulders shook. Probably chuckling at Jonah's obvious discomfort. Malachi grinned. Ruth had chosen well. Corban fit right in with their family. Would Ursula?

As they fought their way through dark caves where groups of angry aliens hid, trying to keep them from returning a crystal to the generator used by the rebel factions to power shields around their cities, Malachi used his speech-to-text program to chat. And to fish. Just a little.

"How'd lunch go?"

Scarlet Fire's avatar executed a flying kick into the face of an alien warrior, and she followed up with a laser blast to his torso. "Good. Appreciate the advice."

"Sure thing." Malachi skirted around a clearly visible tripwire and sidled along the cave wall. Was there any way to ask for more detail without being obvious that he was fishing? "Think you'll do it again?"

She slid along the wall behind him, her laser rifle aimed behind them in case they missed anyone. "If he asks, I'll say yes. But it's his turn now, isn't it?"

Aha. Good to know. And that kind of made sense. Malachi was pretty traditional at heart but had been surprisingly unbothered when she'd asked him out this afternoon. "I guess. Nothing stopping you from asking, is there?"

Using the keyboard, Malachi made his character hunch to avoid the rapidly lowering ceiling. How deep were they going to have to go to make it to the generator? Or had they missed a turn somewhere? No. There, finally, was a light up ahead. They had to be close.

"Trap!" Scarlet Fire's laser blasted past his shoulder just as the boulder in front of them uncurled to reveal an enormous alien that looked like a cross between a troll and a squid.

Malachi switched weapons. His blaster was out of charge and he was down to the tiny pistol that you got when you first created your character. That and—he checked his inventory—six grenades. If they died they'd have to start the whole mission over. He groaned and considered. There. Yes. He tossed a grenade up onto a skinny shelf carved into the roof of the cave. "Look out!"

He turned and ducked behind a rock as the ceiling caved in, trapping the troll-squid-thing beneath it. Scarlet Fire emptied her blaster into the creature's inert form. "Nice. Let's see if we can get this crystal seated and get out."

She didn't seem to be in a hurry to answer his question. It was okay. If it was his turn...well, maybe he'd go ahead and take it.

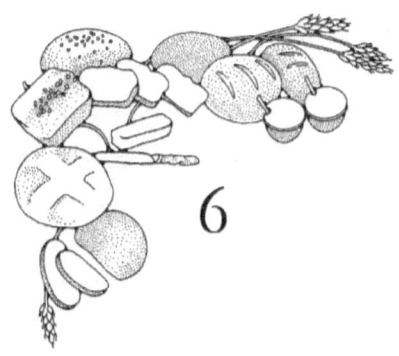

6

Ursula sighed and shut down her computer. Malachi hadn't called. Had their lunch not gone as well as she'd thought? Or had she completely misread his invitation in the first place? Maybe it had been simple friendliness. What if he wasn't attracted to her at all? That'd be pretty much par for the course. Which left her free on Friday night. Again.

She needed to get out of the house. She hadn't left since she got back from lunch on Tuesday. Well, unless walking out to the mailbox counted. She was pretty sure it didn't. Her mother's voice echoed in her head, urging her to get out and make friends. Church. She'd gone to Grace Fellowship on Sunday and hadn't there been something about a movie at the park?

Ursula found her Bible and flipped until she saw where she'd stuffed the bulletin. There it was on the back. Founders Park, just across from the church, at six. That would work. Her stomach sank but she ignored it. She could do this. Maybe even make a friend. Okay, that might be pushing it. But she could get out there and try.

The dinner was ten dollars. She hadn't sent in an RSVP, but surely they'd have extras. And if not, they were close enough to Main that she could grab something from a nearby restaurant. No more excuses. She was going. Tucking her phone into her purse, she stepped out into the warm evening. She'd walk. It was a little farther than she usually trekked, but given how little she'd exercised this week, she needed it.

She gave Mr. Greenway a jaunty wave as she walked by his house. He looked startled to see her out. She needed to get better about exercise. At least get out of the house and enjoy nature when the weather was good. Her parents had always been big after dinner walkers. They'd dragged her along until high school when she put her foot down. Maybe she should resurrect the habit. That would tickle her mom no end.

As she neared the park, a trickle of walkers joined her. Cars were filling the parking lot at the church and families laughed as they gathered picnic baskets and blankets from their trunks. A blanket would've been a good idea. But she'd sat on grass before and could do it again. Especially now that she knew Mom's secret grass-stain removal formula.

A rotund woman manned a table near the start of the food line. "Hi there. You're joining us to eat?"

Ursula nodded. "I'd like to. I didn't call..."

"Oh, that's no problem. We always get walk-ins. Plan for them now." She dimpled and took the ten Ursula offered, giving her a wristband in exchange. "That'll get you your food and a soda. Ice cream too, once they bring that out. Enjoy yourself."

"Thank you." Ursula fumbled with the wristband, trying to wrap it and get the sticky part to adhere to the band, not her arm hair.

"Can I help you with that?" Malachi appeared at her side, his own wrist adorned with the same bright yellow band.

Her heart gave a funny little jump and she held out her arm. "Please. I wasn't expecting to see you."

He gave a one shouldered shrug and jerked his chin at the food line. "We donated the rolls. Jonah and Micah were making rolls all day on top of their usual bread orders. Since all my siblings are here, they sort of roped me into staying. I was ready to give it my best shot at pouting until I spotted you."

"So you're a pouter? That's good to know. I wouldn't have pegged you that way."

"I'm not sure you know me well enough to peg me at all."

He had a point. "Sorry."

Malachi drew his brows together. "I was teasing. I thought you were, too?"

"Yeah. I just...I'm...you know, never mind." Ursula cleared her throat and looked at the line forming at the start of the serving area. No point getting into the whole sordid story of her social ineptitude. "We should go..."

He touched her arm. "Tell me."

She shook her head and turned. "It's not important. Let's eat."

She was halfway to the line when she realized he wasn't beside her. She turned, frowning. He was standing with his hands in his pockets, watching her with confusion written all over his face. She gestured for him to catch up and, after a moment, he strode her way. Weird.

"Hi. Mal-a-chi. I'm. So. Glad. You. Came. Out. Tonight." The woman behind the table offered them paper plates and rolled up plastic ware. "Who. Is. Your. Friend?"

Ursula glanced at Malachi. His cheeks were on fire. Did they think he was slow? Why else would she be talking so loudly and with so much space between each word? "I'm Ursula Franks."

"Oh, honey, you should let him speak for himself. He's not mute. Just deaf." She patted Ursula's hand and shooed them down the table. "You two enjoy now."

Deaf? He was deaf? She looked over to see Malachi intently filling his plate, his expression neutral. Why hadn't he said something? She slid down the line after him, accepting whatever got dumped on her plate by the plastic-gloved workers. At the end of the table, she tugged a can of soda out of one of the coolers filled with ice and met Malachi's gaze. "Where to?"

"Want to join my family?"

She angled her head to the side. Maybe that would give her some insight. "Why not?"

She followed in his wake as he wove through the families who had already arranged themselves on the lawn, her mind still reeling. Some pieces were coming together—questions he hadn't answered because he hadn't been looking at her when she spoke—that sort of thing. She stopped in her tracks. What did it matter? It didn't. Not really. Except for the whole "isn't this something you should mention" aspect.

Ursula recognized his brothers from the bakery and nodded in greeting.

"Guys, you remember Ursula?" Malachi lowered himself to the ground and patted a spot beside him. "And this is my sister's fiancé, Corban DeWitt."

Ursula met Corban's smile. "I've seen you before. Do you have a booth at the farmers market?"

Corban nodded. "Every year. You've been around Arcadia Valley a while, haven't you? Just not Grace?"

She chuckled. "I'm not new to grace, as a concept, but the church, yes. I'm...testing the waters, I guess. I've lived here about five years."

"Well, welcome. Have a seat. How do you know the Baxters?" Corban scooted a bit to make the hole in their circle wider.

"I'm doing the website for the bakery. I also handle Ruth's." Ursula sat and put her plate down in front of her. Grilled chicken rested next to three different kinds of potato salad and a spoonful of coleslaw. She really was distracted if she allowed someone to put coleslaw on her plate. And she'd completely missed the rolls. Her gaze drifted back to the serving line, which had grown since they left it. She wasn't going to get any bread. She sighed.

Malachi nudged her arm. "What's wrong?"

"I missed your contribution to the meal."

He took the roll off his plate and offered it to her. "You can have mine. I know where to get more."

"Thanks." She turned her attention the rest of his family who were all eating and chatting quietly with one another. They were an obvious unit. That had been her impression at the bakery, and sitting here only solidified it. Was there really any hope she could find a place for herself among them? Unlikely. Ursula unrolled her plastic fork and poked at the chicken until she'd peeled off the skin. She could pick it up. The etiquette guide was clear that meat on the bone could be eaten with your fingers. But—her gaze darted to Malachi—how much of a pig did she really want to make of herself?

"Something wrong with your food?" Ruth paused, her piece of chicken halfway to her mouth. "I can run and get you something else. I suspect they'd let me sneak down the back side of the table."

"No, it's fine. I guess I'm not really that hungry." Ursula picked up the bread and tore off a piece.

Malachi seemed to be trying to look everywhere at once. What Ursula had assumed was an extrovert's need to be a part of every conversation. But now? Extrovert certainly didn't seem to fit from the limited time they'd spent together. Lip reading. He was just trying to keep up. It must be exhausting. He caught her watching and heat warmed her cheeks.

He smiled and leaned closer. His breath tickled her cheek as he spoke. "They can be overwhelming, even to me. We don't have to stay with them."

Ursula shook her head. "They're not overwhelming. I just..." She took a deep breath and turned so their eyes met. "The lady at the serving table spilled your secret. And I guess I was wondering why you didn't say anything."

He drew his brows down. "Say anything about what?"

"Being deaf."

Malachi blinked. "I wasn't sure I needed to. Everyone in town seems to know. I appreciated the fact that you didn't make a big deal out of it, though. Not like the ones who talk so loud and slow that I can barely read their lips. I...wasn't trying to hide it."

"You don't sign?" Ursula fiddled with her soda. The conversation was too odd. She'd known deaf people. Columbia, South Carolina, wasn't an enormous city by anyone's standards, but it had enough of a population to have some diversity.

He shrugged. "Sure. Do you?"

"I'm a little rusty." She thought for a moment and signed slowly as she spoke. "The music is too quiet to hear over the crowd."

"She's not wrong." Ruth grinned and stacked Corban's empty plate on top of her own. "Where'd you learn to sign?"

"There was a girl at my middle school. Her family moved halfway through the eighth grade, but before that we'd been friends." Sort of. Back then, Ursula would have said they were with absolute certainty. But now? How did you know, really, what people thought of you? Or maybe she just needed to adjust her definition of friendship.

"Cool." Micah waggled his eyebrows at Malachi and signed something very fast.

Ursula frowned. "That's...unfair."

"And rude." Ruth chimed in, then laughed. "But I don't disagree."

Jonah shook his head and stood, reaching for the stack of empty plates Ruth had made. "Who's rude?"

Ruth flushed. "Sorry. He said—"

Malachi spoke up, signing now as he did, "Nothing important. I heard they were going to have ice cream. You want to go find it with me?"

Clearly Micah had said something about her and no one was going to tell her what. Which probably didn't matter. It might drive her nuts. But she wouldn't let it get to her. She nodded. "Ice cream is always good. But you have to teach me the sign for it while we walk."

He stood and held out his hand, winding his fingers through hers when she would have pulled away. Little shivers ran up her arm. "Okay."

Malachi had held her hand all through the movie—she couldn't remember much about it, she'd been too focused on the sensations of his hand in hers. It was a cartoon with talking animals. She'd gotten that much. And Ruth had signed through the entire thing. Four days later and, if she concentrated, Ursula could still feel his fingers around hers.

He'd walked her home.

They hadn't had much conversation. It had been dark and, well, she'd been content to just be with him. He hadn't seemed to mind. And on the porch, for the briefest of seconds, she'd thought he might kiss her good night. It was too soon. Obviously. But her insides had turned to jelly then, just like they were now. If holding hands could leave her sleepless, what would a kiss do?

With effort, she pulled her thoughts back to her work. The cascading style sheet she used for this particular client wasn't doing the trick. She was going to have to break down and write actual code. Normally that would be the highlight of her day, but it took time to do it right, and she'd been hoping to wander over to the bakery in an hour for lunch. Although...her mother would probably tell her she needed to let him come to her. And she'd been trying to do just that, hadn't she? That's how it was now Tuesday and she hadn't seen him since Friday night.

Oh, he'd texted on Sunday, asking why she hadn't come to church, and he hadn't seemed very happy with her response. But the fact of the matter was that Friday had been an awful lot of interaction for her and she'd still been recovering. She'd spent her time worshipping, as she usually did, with the streaming service of her old church in South Carolina.

And none of this musing was getting her code written. She hunkered down at the keyboard and began to type.

After double-checking that everything worked like she needed it to on the test system she used for projects like this, Ursula uploaded the file to the client's server and, with a quick prayer, set it live. She switched to the client's site in her browser and hit refresh. So far, so good. At least the website was still there. She ran through her test cases and smiled. It worked. She'd send a quick email to the client and then maybe—she paused, was that knocking?

Ursula pushed away from the computer and padded down the hall to the living room. Triton sat in the front window as usual, looking out at the neighborhood. Thinking deep, feline thoughts most likely. She couldn't stop the smile that spread across her face when she spotted Malachi through the glass in the front door. She pulled it open and leaned on the jamb. "Hi there."

"Hi." He took off his sunglasses and hooked them in the front of his baby blue polo. "I was hoping you might be hungry."

"As it turns out, I haven't gotten to lunch yet. Come on in. You're not allergic to cats, are you?" She struggled to recall what might be lurking in her refrigerator. She tended to shop in fits and starts. "I'm not sure what..."

Malachi grinned and held up a reusable grocery bag. "I came prepared. And no. Not to my knowledge."

"Even better. I do have lemonade, if you'd like some?" She closed the door and led the way to the kitchen. Triton hopped out of the window and raced ahead of her. As she walked, she tried to see her place through Malachi's eyes. It was tidy—her mother had drilled that into her too well for it to be otherwise. The furniture was all secondhand, but it was clean and went together relatively well. And, at the end of the day, it all suited her. So she shouldn't worry what he thought. In the kitchen, she pointed to the small table she'd wedged in a corner and went to the fridge for the lemonade pitcher. When she turned for the glasses, he was right there. She swallowed.

"I missed you on Sunday. And hoped all day yesterday you might swing by." He took the pitcher from her and set it on the counter then gently pulled her into his arms, tightening them around her, his cheek resting against her hair.

Ursula's heart sped and she melted into the hug, her own arms slipping around his waist. It might be too soon for a kiss, but this was nearly as potent. Had she ever been hugged like this? Words fought to escape, but there was no point. He wouldn't hear them, couldn't see them. They came out on a sigh as she listened to the strong, steady beat of his heart anyway. "This is nice."

He slowly released her and stepped back, his hands moving as he spoke. "Will you come to church this week? Please?"

She nodded.

"Thank you." He turned and sat at the table, digging into the bag and pulling out one container after another.

Ursula got down two glasses and filled them. She put the pitcher back in the fridge and carried the drinks over. "What did you bring? It smells amazing."

"Jonah's a chef, not just a baker. In D.C, he was one or two steps down from the top at a pretty upscale restaurant. I don't know the official chef terms, but whatever. He cooks really well. And he likes it. So even though he's up at dawn baking these days, he's usually game to make supper. Or help out with some special treats when his brother asks." Malachi peeled the lids off the containers, letting even more of the fragrant aromas into the air. "Corban keeps bringing Ruth vegetables. Since it makes her—and Jonah—happy, I can't complain too much. But the consequence is that it's basically all vegetarian in here. Ratatouille, some kind of pesto over fresh angel hair, and a zucchini and squash casserole that is surprisingly good."

"I'll get plates." She paused and touched his arm. "Thanks, Malachi. This is...special."

He grinned.

When she'd returned with plates and forks, she sat. "Maybe...you could sign a blessing?"

His eyebrows lifted but he gave a short nod and bowed his head. She watched his hands, their fluid motion as they spoke gratitude for the food and...for her?

She echoed his amen and reached for the nearest container. "How's the bakery?"

He shrugged and scooped food onto his own plate. "Okay. It's a challenge, at times, because our focus is bread. I mean, that's the point of a community supported bakery. But people assume we have cakes and éclairs and, I don't know, fruit tarts. And Jonah could make all those things, but with another bakery already in town—one that does have those things—it seems silly to duplicate them. Plus, Mrs. Delis is nice, so I'd hate to harm her business."

The woman was nice. Ursula frequented Demi's Delights at least once every couple of weeks for their fantastic coffee, and to force herself to leave the house. "How do you avoid that though?"

"As a community supported bakery, we shouldn't really have a problem. The bulk of our business is subscription-based. People sign up to receive a certain number of loaves of bread a week. We have the storefront, sure, but honestly that decision was more about having an easy place for customers to pick up their shares and a good commercial kitchen than anything else. The handful of walk-in business we get is a bonus."

"You're using completely local ingredients too, though, right?"

"Not everything. The flour, yes. And oats. Jonah tracked down someone near enough who can supply us there. But there's no local source for asiago cheese and olives."

"Still. It's a selling point." She chuckled. He certainly wasn't winning any self-promotion awards. But that kind of worked in his favor. At least to her.

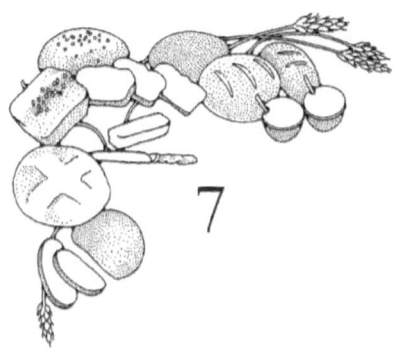

7

"How'd it go?" Jonah paused in the process of measuring out flour as Malachi came back into the kitchen. "She like the food?"

"You outdid yourself. It was great." Malachi continued toward the office, still not sure what to make of things. They'd had good conversation. But it was all superficial. Mostly about the bakery and things they could try working in that wouldn't necessarily be competition with Demi's Delights. He'd wanted to know about her. But every time he'd tried to shift conversation in that direction, she'd deflected.

Jonah touched his shoulder. "What's up?"

Malachi shrugged. He didn't want to get into it. Not yet. He needed some time to think it through on his own.

"Okay. But if you change your mind and want to talk, you know I'm here, right?"

"Right."

"And I do know a tiny bit more about the female of the species, having been close to marriage at one point in my life."

Malachi shook his head. Neither he nor Micah would've let Jonah go through with that. She was a nightmare and Jonah was the only one who hadn't seen it. "Narrow escape."

"True. But still." Jonah sent him a concerned look.

"Thanks." Malachi closed the office door behind him and collapsed into the chair. She seemed interested...she'd certainly appeared to enjoy the hug. But then, it was like she pulled away and tucked all the real pieces of herself out of reach. He sighed. Which was the real Ursula? The flesh and blood woman he'd held in his arms, or the electronic one he connected with on every non-physical level online? How could he be halfway in love with one and completely confused by the other?

He checked the email. Two new subscriptions from folks in Twin Falls. They were going to have to figure out delivery sooner than later. For now, people who wanted fresh, local bread were willing to drive. But in the grand scheme, it made more sense to set up delivery days. He didn't mind driving and it was a better use of his time than sitting in the office doing non-existent paperwork. Now that the bulk of the processes were in place, he just had to update the finances and stay on top of little details. It wasn't a full-time job.

Since he had no desire to get roped into helping in the kitchen, he needed to figure out ways to be useful. Delivery service might just fit the bill. He pulled up a map on the computer and scrolled around. At least this, unlike Ursula, was a problem he could solve.

Jonah snagged Malachi's sleeve. "Before you sneak upstairs to do...whatever it is you're on your computer 'til all hours doing, can we have a business meeting of sorts?"

Malachi swallowed his irritation at missing out on the possibility of connecting with Ursula in the game and nodded. "Kitchen?"

"Micah's in the living room. Ruth's on her way over."

Ruth was coming? She had very little to do with the CSB these days. Hadn't since she'd been able to re-open the Fairview shortly after he'd arrived in town. She was an interested party on the business loan, so it made sense. Probably. He padded into the living room and snagged the free recliner. At least this way he could go over his proposal for deliveries in Twin Falls while everyone was around. He should go get his laptop. He popped the footrest back down and stood.

Micah looked up from his cell phone. "Where are you going?"

"Grab my laptop. Be right back."

Micah shrugged and returned his attention to his phone.

Malachi took the stairs two at a time. In his room, he detached his laptop from the dock that tied in his monitor, keyboard, and mouse when he was at his desk. He didn't have a full proposal worked up yet. But it wasn't as if his brothers cared about having a slide show with charts. He had enough information to show the usefulness, and it wasn't likely to be a hard sell anyway. All three—four, really—Baxters wanted to do whatever they had to in order to make the CSB a success.

Back in the living room, he frowned. Jonah had snagged the other recliner, leaving him with a spot on the couch. Whoever had bought that couch clearly hadn't sat on it before buying it. Oh well. It'd be hard to show things on his laptop from the recliner anyway.

Ruth smiled from the other end of the couch. "There you are. I don't have a lot of time, Corban's keeping an eye on the B&B. We're full up and there are always folks who need a pot of tea, some cookies, or directions in the evening."

"Can't Corban handle that?" Jonah frowned.

Malachi snickered. That had been his thought as well. If anyone could give directions, it was probably going to be the man who'd lived in the area basically his whole life. But whatever. His sister was protective— determined to make a success of the place on her own. Letting someone help...he didn't have grounds to say anything. He wasn't exactly the poster child for admitting he needed it, either.

"Oh hush. Both of you. And you, too." She pinned Micah with her gaze.

He held up his hands. "What'd I do?"

"You thought too loud. I heard it. And yes, I realize I'm over protective and that Corban can handle things. Can we just get on with it, please?" She smiled sweetly and fluttered her eyelashes.

"That hasn't worked on any of us for years. But yeah, let's get started." Jonah cleared his throat. "I wanted to talk to you about the idea of expanding our offerings a little."

Malachi pursed his lips.

"Really? What happened to not competing with the other place in town?" Micah raised the foot on the recliner where he sat. "Arcadia Valley isn't that big. Two bakeries?"

"That's the thing. They don't have some of the things that we could offer. Bread, for example, wasn't something they had. Then you throw in cupcakes, cookies, muffins, and maybe donuts. Bagels? We stick close to the bread idea, but expand a bit. I'm not interested in becoming a pastry chef or a cake decorator. I mean, I can, but that's not what I love. I suspect we might even find customers want the subscription model for some of those items, too." Jonah leaned forward, his elbows on his knees, expression earnest.

"Hmm." Ruth tapped her lower lip. "The grocery store has all of those things."

"True. But not locally sourced. And if we look for a good, fair trade supplier for chocolate, we can do more than oatmeal cookies. Or at least add chocolate chips to them." Jonah's glance moved between each of his siblings.

Malachi considered. It was reasonable. They had the storefront already. They weren't doing a booming walk-in business, except for folks coming by to pick up their shares each week. Having impulse items like cookies and muffins available wasn't a bad idea. If you were there for two loaves of bread, it was unlikely you'd randomly decide to buy a third. But a dozen cookies? "I like it."

"Really?" Ruth looked surprised. "Of all of us, I thought you'd be the least likely to see this as a good idea. It's a risk, financially. Isn't it?"

Malachi shook his head. "Not really. The only added cost is more ingredients. So we should move slowly, small batches until we see how they sell. But the overhead stays the same. Basically. We'll have to check with Ben at Corinna's Cupboard to make sure he's okay if we end up adding more donations to the current box of day olds we give him. But I can't really see him having a problem with that. He said it's only because they were completely privately funded that he was able to accept food that didn't come in a sealed container with an expiration stamped on it. But since he can, what's the problem with a little more—or a little extra variety?"

"You're sure?" Micah eyed Malachi. "'Cause if you are, I'm for it. We've had a couple people ask about different items and I've always said we could do special order, but when they hear that, I think they just hear a cash register in their head."

Ruth laughed. "Probably. All right. If you three think it's a good idea, then go for it. And I'll be on my way."

"Hold up." Malachi opened up his laptop and leaned forward. "Since we're all here, I have something we need to discuss, too."

Ruth sat back down.

"Uh-oh." Jonah eyed the computer. "It's never good when he breaks that thing out."

"We need to consider delivering to Twin Falls."

Micah shook his head. "We talked about that when we started. Between the farmers market and the store, people know where to come."

"If we're billing ourselves as local and eco-friendly, then it doesn't make a ton of sense to be driving all over creation." Jonah tented his fingers. "Why do you bring it up?"

"Because we're getting more enrollments from folks in the city every day. If that's the number of people who are willing to drive, you have to figure there are at least a few more who want to do it but can't work it into their schedule. And if we raise the fee slightly to cover gas, some might still choose to pick up, but I kind of doubt it." Malachi opened the document he'd been working on comparing the prices and delivery structure for community supported bakeries in similar-sized areas. "Here."

Micah took the laptop and looked it over, a slight frown creasing his forehead. "This is current?"

Malachi nodded.

Micah passed the computer to Jonah who smiled as he read it. "You're always so thorough. You really think we need this now? Not some unforeseen point in the future?"

"I do. We want to grow. It's going to be easier to do that if we're flexible and available everywhere. If we want to talk about expanding into some of the communities to the north and west, those can probably wait. But we're close enough to Twin Falls that I think it's better to let them know we want to serve them and will work to make it convenient. Plus, if we're talking about a lower environmental impact, one person going down to Twin Falls is better than eight making the round trip." Malachi signed rapidly while he spoke, then dropped his hands into his lap. "Ruth?"

She nodded. "It doesn't hurt to try. We can always stop if in, say, six months, it's not an appreciable increase. How will you work in the new menu items with delivery?"

That was an interesting question. It wasn't one he'd considered since that hadn't been on the table when he tackled the problem this afternoon. But...he'd been planning to have a little extra with him on deliveries. "I'll just take some along. I've been thinking we need to do a weekly newsletter for our subscribers anyway. So I can let them know ahead of time—if you let me know—what flavors we're looking at. They can either send in an additional order or bank on having a small supply available."

"Newsletter? Dude. Who's doing that?" Jonah crossed his arms.

"Me. Chill. All you have to do is tell me what you've got in terms of flavors. If they're not going to change weekly or seasonally then you only need to do that once. But I was thinking..."

Micah shook his head. "That's never good."

"Hush. Both of you." Ruth reached over and set the laptop next to Malachi. "Go on."

He took a deep breath. He did more than keep the books. Did his brothers not understand that he had ideas, too? "All right. What do we sell most of?"

"The sandwich loaf. Followed probably by the asiago." Jonah chewed his lip. "Maybe the olive. Why?"

"Those are staples, right? But if we do seasonal loaves—or muffins, whatever. Like right now, Corban's talking about how he's being overrun by zucchini, and so is everyone else, so his stall at the farmers market isn't selling them as fast as he'd like. What if we bought it and did zucchini bread and muffins through August?"

Ruth frowned. "If they're all overrun with their own, why would they buy our bread?"

"Because they don't have to make it." Malachi sighed. "Do you remember Mom stopped planting it because she couldn't use it fresh fast enough but she was too busy to do the processing and make bread to freeze?"

"That's true, she did." Micah rubbed his nose. "And pumpkin in the fall."

"Right." Malachi gave a half-smile. "But what if we expanded that idea further. Jonah, you want to experiment with other flavors, right?"

Jonah nodded.

"So you can do that on a small-scale basis. We advertise it as a limited time thing to get people to add it to their orders and because we're not necessarily going to make it permanent, if people don't love it after the first buy, it's not as big a deal." Malachi watched the thoughts flit across his brothers' faces. They were hesitant. Jonah clearly liked the idea. It gave him the chance to experiment some. He'd been missing that. But Micah was struggling.

"I like the idea. Especially since you're picking up the extra work." Jonah grinned.

"All right. If you're sure." Micah shrugged. "I'm not going to stand in the way."

"It's not like we have to do it forever." Ruth looked at Malachi. "Right? If it doesn't work, we reevaluate."

He nodded. That was always the case, no matter what the idea.

"Okay. Do it. The newsletter thing—when do you want to start that?" Jonah rubbed the back of his neck.

"Monday? Get me your menu for the week by Sunday night? That gives us four days—the rest of this week—to soft-launch the new items in the store. And delivery, plus new items, will go into the first newsletter next week." Malachi held his breath. It was fast. Faster than either of his brothers usually moved. Except this whole CSB had been one quick decision after another, and so far, they were working. He knew he did a lot of praying about their venture. His brothers and sister probably did too. But they'd made that first step out in faith. It only made sense to keep walking.

"Done. Go play with your imaginary girlfriend. I know we're keeping you from her. Although...does she know you're stepping out on her? With a real, live woman?" Jonah smiled.

"You're just jealous." Malachi ignored the tiny barb in Jonah's words. His friends weren't imaginary. Just because he didn't know any of them in person—well, now he knew one, but she didn't know that—didn't mean they weren't real people. Or real friends. "And it's hard to step out on someone if you're not dating in the first place."

"Oh please." Micah shook his head. "You spend practically every night together. How is that not dating?"

"It's called friendship." Malachi frowned.

"That's right. And it's what you have with Ursula, too. Or you're working on it. Leave him be, guys." Ruth stood. "I've got to get back."

Jonah craned his neck, his gaze following Ruth as she left. He turned back to Malachi. "I'm still with Micah. You're totally dating the red flame girl. If she's even a girl."

Micah laughed and slapped his knee. "Wouldn't that be something? Mal falling in love with a guy online. Maybe it's good you have a policy against meeting online friends in real life."

"Scarlet Flame, and I can guarantee you, she's a woman."

"Yeah? How?" Jonah raised his eyebrows.

"Because I've met her. And so have you." Malachi took a deep breath, relaxing some as his brothers' faces showed confusion. "I'm pretty sure it's Ursula."

Jonah's mouth dropped open into a little "O."

"No way." Micah shook his head. "She seems entirely too normal to be a gamer. Why would you think that?"

"Too many little coincidences." Malachi grabbed his laptop and stood. "'Night."

"No way. Sit back down and explain yourself." Jonah pointed to the couch. "This is huge. Is that why you didn't want to talk after lunch?"

Malachi lifted a shoulder and perched on the arm of the couch. He filled his brothers in about the little connections that had made it clear, at least in his mind, that Scarlet Fire and Ursula were one and the same.

"Wow." Micah rubbed the back of his neck. "That's... Seriously, what are the odds?"

Jonah shook his head. "I can't fault your logic, but like Micah said, those are some long odds. You're sure?"

"As sure as I can be."

"What are you going to do about it?"

Malachi frowned at Jonah. "What do you mean?"

"Oh, come on. I know we tease you, but you can't deny you're at least half in love with Scarlet Fire. Which means you're half in love with Ursula. Who you are now in a position to date." Jonah leaned forward and propped his elbows on his knees. "So...?"

"So I'm going to get to know the real her and see where that takes us."

"But you're going to tell her? You have to." Micah glanced at Jonah. "He has to, right?"

Jonah shrugged.

Did he? Probably. But what on earth would that conversation look like? "I guess."

"Bro." Jonah pointed his finger at Malachi. "Do it sooner than later. Nothing good ever comes from trying to hide something in a relationship. Take it from me."

Malachi nodded, though it hadn't been Jonah who'd been hiding something. Still, the advice was sound. But...the question still remained: how did he bring it up? And what happened if he was wrong?

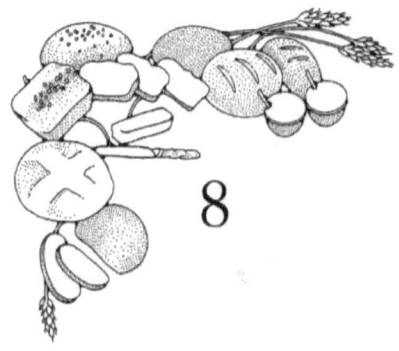

8

Bleary-eyed, Ursula poured another steaming mug of coffee, added a generous splash of half-and-half, and stirred in a packet of sweetener. She'd stayed up entirely too late last night playing Orion's Quest. But MalRen had been determined to finish the Zerillanskan mission, and some of the bonuses had been too good to pass up. She was going to pay for it today. Thankfully, she had very little maintenance work to do, so she could devote the bulk of the day to the bakery website. She'd like to have it done by the end of next week. They didn't want anything that was particularly challenging, so there was very little reason for her to be taking as long as she was. Was she just trying to drag out the association with Malachi?

She wiggled her mouse to wake her computer and, with one leg tucked under her, opened her email. Triton hopped up on the desk and settled into the cat bed she had for him where most people would put an in box. She rubbed the cat's head before smiling. Speaking of Malachi, what did his email have to say? Her eyebrows rose as she read over the needed changes and additions. Still nothing major, but this took it to the next level. It was nice to see that they were going to have more than a basic information dump as their website. And muffins? Her mouth watered. Maybe she'd wander over that way today after all.

What was she going to do when their website was finished and she didn't have an excuse to stop by? Not that grabbing a loaf of bread wasn't an excuse, but she didn't need to do that every day. Even with their expanded menu, she wouldn't need to go that way very often. Her heart twanged and her thoughts drifted back to their hug. Was it possible there could be more?

Her cell chirped with an incoming text. Maybe he *was* thinking of her.

"R U busy tonight?"

She tapped back a negative.

"Want 2 be?"

"Sure. What do u have in mind?"

"Dinner?"

"What time?"

"5:30 – I'll pick u up."

"Sounds good."

Ursula spun in her chair, grinning. A date. There was no other word for it. She grabbed her cell and tapped her mom's number.

"Hi, sweetie. You're calling early. Everything okay?"

She pressed a hand to her jumping stomach. "Yep. I just got asked out on a date."

"Malachi?"

"Yes. Not just bumping into each other at a church thing. He texted."

There was a pause. "He asked you out via text? He couldn't just pick up the phone?"

Ursula drew her lower lip between her teeth. "I'm not sure how that would work. I...guess I forgot to mention that he's deaf?"

"Oh. Well. There's that typing thing for phones, right? And I'm pretty sure there are programs in place— relays or something—so you can still talk to someone who has one without having to have one yourself. But...in this case, I'll forgive the text. Do you need me to ship your ASL books out? I think I know where they are."

Ursula chuckled. Her mom always rolled with the punches. They had their differences like every mother and daughter, but whenever she heard other people talking about their nightmare parents, she was always grateful God had given her the set she had. "You know what, that's not a bad idea. I've been brushing up a little online, but the books are probably more convenient. Do you mind?"

"Not at all. It'll give me a reason to get your father off the computer and out of the house. He says he's close to defeating the Vogons or something and doesn't want to stop until he does."

"Ashkors?"

"I don't know. Sure. That makes as much sense as what I said. What is *wrong* with the two of you? Maybe having an actual date will get you offline a little."

She chuckled. Given that she'd gotten two glimpses now of Malachi shrinking a game, that wasn't as likely as her mom thought. But it might change *what* game she was playing. No need to disabuse her of that notion though. Not yet. "We'll see. Anyway, I just wanted to say thank you for pushing me to try a local church."

"I'm just glad you finally did it. Although, from what you said, starting much sooner wouldn't have let you meet this young man anyway. He's new to the area?"

"Right." That was a good point. And it eased the fingers of guilt that had been trying to worm their way in. "But I'm still glad you pushed."

"No matter how old you get, I'll always be your mother."

"True. Love you, Mom."

"Love you, too. Get to work. And let me know how things go."

Ursula ended the call and opened up the files she'd been working on for the bakery. If she could get it working well enough to upload to her test server, she could walk over and pull it up for them to look at. And maybe snag a muffin. Or was that too much if they had a date tonight anyway?

A date. She grinned. Now just had to figure out how to keep from messing it up like she usually did.

Ursula wiggled into the floaty blue and white skirt and tugged on a pale yellow top with a gathered scoop neck. She frowned at her reflection in the mirror. It was summery but...too casual? Too dressy? Ugh. A glance at the clock showed that she had about five minutes. Whatever it was, she was wearing it. She slid into a pair of semi-dressy sandals, grabbed her purse, and leaned closer to the mirror to swipe gloss over her lips as the doorbell rang. That would have to do.

She opened the door and stopped, catching her breath. "Wow."

Red stained his cheeks, but he smiled. "I could say the same. I brought you these."

Ursula took the sunny gerbera daisies and sniffed. They were wrapped in the distinctive paper of Blossoms by the Akers. Her eyebrows lifted. Classy. "These are lovely. Come in, will you? I want to put these in water. Do we have time?"

He nodded. "There's no rush."

After hesitating for a moment, Ursula stepped in, wrapped her arms around him and squeezed. Leaning back so he could see her lips, she said, "Thank you."

Heat warming her cheeks at her brash action, she turned and strode to the kitchen. Triton looked up briefly from his dinner bowl then continued munching. She took her grandma's Waterford vase down from the top of the fridge and rinsed it before filling it with water and dumping in the fertilizer packet that was rubber banded around the bottom of the daisy stems. She quickly snipped the ends and dropped the flowers into the vase with a promise to do a better job arranging them soon.

"You're good at that."

She started and turned. "Dad brings my mom flowers every week. She's big on seeing how long they can last. The key, she says, is plant food and trimming the stems. I guess we'll see."

Malachi nodded and held out his hand. "Ready?"

Her tongue darted between her lips as she clasped his hand. "Yes."

Electricity sizzled up her arm. It wasn't unpleasant. If anything, it made her hyper-aware of their points of contact. Outside on the porch, she checked the door and paused when she saw his car.

"I thought we could head into Twin Falls and see what there is to see."

"That sounds...perfect. It's such a nice town. Do you get down there often?"

He shook his head and held open her door. "Nope. But that'll be changing next week. In fact...do you mind if we scout out one spot?"

"No. Spot for what?"

He held up a finger before closing her door and rounding the car. Seated in the driver's chair, he turned so he could see her. "We're starting deliveries once a week. I've been on the phone most of the day tracking down a parking lot that doesn't mind me setting up shop, so to speak, for an hour or so one day a week. It's easier if people come to pick up from a central location rather than driving all over town to do deliveries at their homes. Plus with weather and so forth, I'm not sure how we'd work out the logistics of keeping the bread safe. But if they know I'll be at the back of the parking lot at Main and Gooding at a certain time, it's easier for them to get over and collect and save themselves the trouble of driving into Arcadia Valley."

"Smart."

He grinned and started the engine. "I thought so. My brothers took some convincing. So I guess we'll see how it pays off."

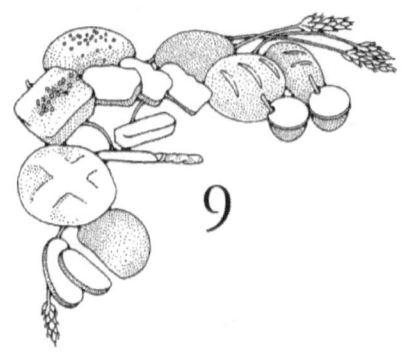

9

The parking lot was perfect for setting up a pickup location. And so was walking, hand in hand, with Ursula. Since they were right in the middle of downtown, it made sense to leave the car and stroll. She'd said she wasn't starving yet, so they could browse Main and see if something struck their fancy. He chuckled to himself as Ursula tugged her hand free and worked to sign while she talked. It was sweet. And so he signed in return, even though the other people on the street were obviously trying not to stare.

"Doesn't it bother you?"

Ursula looked confused. "What?"

"People are gawking. At us." Malachi checked the traffic at the stop sign and tugged her into the crosswalk.

"So? It's probably because you're so handsome." Her hand flew to her mouth as the words finished. Red spread across her cheeks.

Malachi grinned. "Am I now?"

She jabbed his ribs with her elbow. "Now that we've accomplished your mission to find a good, central location for Slice of Heaven pickups, you said something about dinner?"

"I did. Let's see what sounds good." Now his cheeks heated. "Should I have chosen something and planned on it? I'm...rusty when it comes to dates. I'm sorry."

"Don't be. How rusty?"

When they reached the curb, Malachi glanced down the street. It was pathetic. She'd laugh. And then...he shook his head and pointed. "What's that?"

A slight frown marring her expression, Ursula followed his pointing finger. "Oh fun. There's live music. The banner..." She squinted, raising a hand to shade her eyes. "Looks like it's an every Wednesday thing in the summer. Do you want...never mind. That was dumb."

"We can, if you want to? I don't mind."

Ursula shook her head. "Doesn't start for another hour. And it wouldn't be any fun for you, would it? Let's just find dinner."

They strolled along, looking at the store fronts. There was only one sandwich shop and a sushi place before they'd gone three blocks. Malachi stopped. "This is ridiculous. I should've planned better. I'm sorry. Why don't we head back to the car and we can look something up."

"It's okay. I enjoyed the walk." She pressed her lips together. "You know what I could really go for?"

"What?"

"Mexican."

He pulled his cell phone out of his pocket and opened a browser. There were several choices, but the car was probably still the first place to start. He tipped the screen toward her. "Choose what sounds good."

She dragged the map with one finger until Arcadia Valley came back into view and tapped on a purple dot. "This one."

His heart sank. She wanted to head back home. It was probably some hole in the wall that would get them in and out in ten minutes. Tacos that were a shaky step up from Taco Bell. Not that he'd eaten at a Taco Bell in a while. But still. He gave himself a firm mental kick. He was going to have to refresh himself on dating protocol. Provided Ursula gave him another chance. And that didn't seem overly likely. "Okay. You're sure you don't want to stay in town?"

Something in his tone must have given away how he felt. Ursula stopped and stepped in front of him, her gaze locked to his. "I just want to be with you. I'm out of practice myself. I think the last date I went on was at Christmas when my mom set me up with the visiting son of a friend of hers from church. It...did not go well. This is already so much better. I like the food at El Corazon and, last time I was there, they mentioned they might be transitioning to a more farm-to-table menu. I don't know for sure if they've done that yet, but even if they haven't, it'll be a good meal."

His spirit lightened a fraction. Maybe...maybe this wasn't a complete disaster after all. He nodded. "Okay."

Ursula's lips twitched and she raised her chin, leaning forward to brush her mouth to his. Malachi froze, the air clogging in his chest. Tiny bolts of electricity skimmed through him at her brief touch.

He swallowed. He should say something. Anything. But there were no words left in his brain. She was watching him. Waiting? Hand trembling, he brushed a strand of hair away from her cheek and, his eyes searching hers, brought their lips together once again.

"You're awfully cheerful for someone who's looking at a spreadsheet." Jonah dropped into the chair next to Malachi's desk and chugged from a water bottle. "You can't possibly know how well the muffins and cookies are doing already, can you?"

Malachi shook his head but couldn't keep the grin off his face even if he wanted to. Which he decidedly did not.

"I take it the date went well?"

"Had some great Mexican food. We should go as a family. You know how Micah loves good shredded beef."

"Mmmhmm. Where is this shredded beef that put you in such a good mood?"

"The rice was good, too. El Corazon."

Jonah snickered. "My Spanish might be a little rusty, but I'm pretty sure it's the restaurant's namesake, not their food, that's got you in a good mood."

Malachi lifted a shoulder. His brother was right, his heart *was* responsible for the good mood. Of course he was. But there was no need to encourage the knowing, slightly smug, gleam in his eye. "Did you need me?"

"Nope. Just taking a break. Although...if you're hungry, I have a new recipe coming out of the oven in about five. Wanna taste test for me?"

"Sure, bring it in when it's ready." He turned back to the spreadsheet. He'd emailed all of the Twin Falls customers individually. The response to the pickup location was overwhelmingly positive. Now he just had to get the time figured out. For those it absolutely didn't work for, he could possibly arrange to-the-door delivery for a higher fee. But he'd rather avoid that if he could. While he didn't mind driving, you couldn't leave bread sitting on someone's front step for very long and still guarantee it tasted the way you intended. Even in plastic, it could end up dried out or soggy or just...off. And that said nothing about animals. Better to control the conditions as much as possible.

Malachi hit *save* and closed out the customer list. They'd probably need to upgrade to a database. Sooner rather than later, as it was always easier to migrate small quantities of data than big ones. And it really seemed like things were going to take off. The bonus of being a CSB instead of a CSA was the year-round nature. They weren't really dependent on crops. Sure, the wheat, oats, whatever all grew in the summer, but they kept well enough with the right storage techniques. And since Jonah only ground the flour as they needed it, they didn't have to worry about that spoiling, even though they weren't adding preservatives to it. It was more labor intensive, but anyone who tasted their products could tell the difference, even if they didn't know exactly what they were tasting.

He drummed his fingers on the desk. A database. The website would probably have a database on the back end for the online sign ups. Was it possible to have it go directly into the same one that he'd use and save a step? He'd never seen Ruth moving information from the online reservations to her reservation system. But was that because it was a professional product? Or could Ursula tie into something he put together? The only way to find out was to ask. He typed out a quick email and sent it. No point struggling through a database design until he knew the answer. Or maybe there was a product that would do what they needed...he'd research that.

"Here we go." Jonah came back in with a steaming muffin on a plate. "Don't be shy, okay? Like I said, it's an experiment."

Malachi sniffed the warm, nutty steam that rose from the treat. His mouth watered. He broke it in half and sniffed again. Why did he smell apples? He bit into one half and chewed thoughtfully. Oats, definitely apple of some sort and... "Are those hazelnuts?"

"I should've known you'd figure it out. Micah had no idea. Good?"

Malachi nodded. "Where are the apples from?"

"Caught that, too? It's applesauce, but yeah. There's a good apple growing region—small—near Boise.

I figure grown in Idaho probably still counts as local. Or at least local-ish. After all, I still have to get some of the savory ingredients from organic wholesalers. The filberts are local, too."

"Huh. It's good. That's today's flavor?" Malachi polished off the first half of the muffin and bit into the second. "Could use a touch of butter."

Jonah nodded. "That's what Micah said, too. And no. Tomorrow, I think. Speaking of that..."

Malachi cocked his head to the side.

"Seems to me a weekly flavor makes more sense all around. Commit to something for six days."

"Why?" Malachi finished the muffin and reached for the cup of cold coffee that sat next to his computer monitor.

"Lot of reasons. First off, your newsletter. What if Twin Falls folks want a flavor but it doesn't happen to be on delivery day? Kind of stinks to be them. And us. 'Cause we're losing out on their add-on business and if that happens too many times, I'm not sure they'll stick around."

"That's fair. What else?"

Jonah flipped the cap back down on his water bottle. "Next biggest is ordering. Easier to order a week at a time than a day. We'll get better breaks for the bulk that way, too."

"Okay. Weekly it is."

"That was easy." Jonah punched Malachi's arm. "Micah said you were going to give me a hard time about it."

"Why?"

"Dunno. He's in a mood." Jonah checked his watch and stood. "Gotta run."

Malachi frowned, his gaze darting to the clock on his monitor. Then he chuckled. Almost three. He could stand to stretch his legs. It was always entertaining to watch his brother pour on the charm.

Pushing through the swinging door that led to the front of the bakery, he fought a smile. The woman was like clockwork. Plus she teetered on the edge of gorgeous, and the standard blue police uniform couldn't do anything to change that. She didn't appear to notice it. She breezed into the bakery and stopped, as she always did, to close her eyes and breathe deeply.

"Hey, guys. Wow. You're all out front today? Slow day in the kitchen?"

Jonah turned and frowned at Malachi before stuffing his hands into his pockets. "I guess those two decided to take their break out front. How's your day, Officer Sinclair?"

"You can call me Gloria, Jonah. I promise not to leave a review online saying you're overly friendly with your clientele. Though that might be a bonus in some folks' minds. It's been...pretty low key. So I guess that's a good day. What do you have that's new? I'm feeling adventurous."

Malachi ducked back into the kitchen and scanned the area where Jonah usually set items to cool. Aha. There were the oat-nut muffins. He snagged two and set them on a plate, carrying them out front. He tapped Jonah on the shoulder and handed him the plate.

"What are those?" Gloria leaned across the counter and sniffed. "They smell amazing."

Red crawled up Jonah's neck. "I'm not sure they're ready yet. They're just something I've been playing with..."

"Nope." She wiggled her fingers. "Hand 'em over."

"I..." Jonah cast Micah a helpless look.

Micah shrugged and rang up two muffins.

"Don't charge her. Geez." Jonah pushed the plate across the top of the display case. "On the house. I'm told they need butter. We aren't set up with those little packets yet though. They're still on order. The whole muffin and cookie thing is a recent and rather spontaneous decision."

Gloria beamed. "Those are usually the best kinds. You're sure I can't pay? I'm positive I'm going to enjoy these."

"I'm sure." Jonah sent Micah a pointed look.

Micah huffed out a sigh and voided the transaction.

"Well. Thank you." She angled her head to the side. "Care to join me?"

Malachi tugged on Micah's sleeve and nodded toward the kitchen.

"What did he say?" Malachi crossed to the muffins and tossed one to his twin.

"I don't know, you dragged me out of there too fast for me to catch it. Hopefully, he'll realize someone has to be out there and I am now, officially, on break." Micah crossed to the office and flopped into the extra chair. "How was the date last night?"

Malachi fought the urge to roll his eyes. Sure, it had been a long time—like high school—since he'd asked someone out. That didn't mean he wanted to dissect every little thing with someone. "Good. What'd you do?"

"Went to bed early. Earlier. This schedule...we may have to rethink how long we're open every day."

Malachi nodded. "What if we opened later? We aren't getting the early morning crowd like we originally expected. If we opened at say, nine, you could get here to start baking at six, maybe even seven. 'Cause you just need the first batch of orders to be ready for the folks who pick up in the morning. We basically know who that is at this point. Most people are picking up in the afternoon on their way home from work. No one really wants to have their bread sitting in the car all day."

"That's a thought. But if we decide to add donuts, those are a morning impulse. You don't think they'll draw an earlier crowd?"

It was possible. On the other hand, it might not. Some are likely to be just as happy to buy a box of donuts the night before. It wasn't as if they'd be stale in twelve hours. He shrugged. "Better to change the hours now and just have people work around it, than to end up with a morning crowd and two bakers who are dead on their feet."

"Or you could take the whole shooting match on at say, one, and Jonah and I could go home and nap."

Malachi scoffed. "Right. Like Jonah's going to miss out on Gloria every day?"

Micah grinned. "You have a point."

Malachi stretched out on his bed with his laptop and logged into Orion's Quest, eager to see Ursula again, even if it was only her alter ego. He was halfway through a negotiation for an engine upgrade when her chat request came though.

"Got a second?"

"Gimme one—need to finish this." Malachi frowned at the price. He could probably get the guy down another thousand credits, but how long would it take? He had the money. Fine. He accepted and transferred the in-game cash. The upgrade would be installed on his ship in three hours. Most days, the fact that they tried to make the game more realistic with wait times for certain upgrades was annoying. But tonight...well he could just chat with Ursula. He typed back. "Okay. I'm here. What's up?"

"You're a guy, right? IRL?"

He frowned. Did she really not recognize who he was? Or was she joking around? Either way, he could play. "Yes. Why?"

"Need advice from a guy perspective."

"Shoot."

"If a girl kisses you, does it bother you that she made the first move?"

Malachi shook his head. "Nope."

"You're sure?"

"Did he not kiss you back? Or wipe his mouth after or something that made you think this?" Malachi pulled his lip between his teeth. Had he messed up somewhere?

"No. Nothing like that. I just...it's more forward than I've ever been."

"Pretty sure it's not a problem."

"Do you really think that's the general feeling amongst guys?"

"Seriously? Yeah. Takes the pressure off. Unless you kissed him and don't ever want to do it again. That would be a bummer." He held his breath as he hit enter. Two could play this game.

"Ha ha. Definitely not the case. Just worried I might have messed everything up."

"Guarantee you didn't."

"Blaming you if it turns out you're wrong."

He grinned. No chance of that. "Fair enough. What mission are you on?"

Their talk turned to the game and snippets—generic ones—about their day. Malachi offered a silent prayer of thanks that she'd asked. And that she appeared to take him at face value. But still...he pulled his phone out of his pocket and opened a new text.

"Hey. Thinking of you. Had a good time last night. Grinned all day."

There. That ought to put her mind at ease. In the game, Ursula stopped mid-story about one of her web clients and said she had to run. A minute later, his phone chimed with an incoming text. Malachi set his computer aside. Maybe this was better.

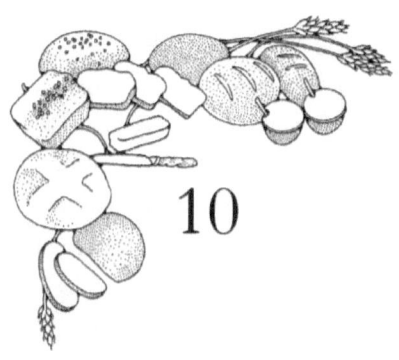

# 10

Ursula clutched her Bible to her chest and scanned the crowd in the foyer. Grace Fellowship wasn't large...how was she missing Malachi? A woman in her mid-to-late forties hurried toward her, a grin on her face. Was she the welcome wagon? Not that that was bad, but...Ursula's stomach tightened. It always seemed so awkward and forced.

Malachi's arm came around her shoulder and he kissed her cheek before signing hello. "Sorry I'm late."

Ursula turned to face him. "It's okay. But I was starting to worry."

Malachi moved his arm and signed without speaking. "Sorry. I saw Mrs. Poncetta heading for you and got here as fast as I could."

"She's not nice?" Ursula signed, her gaze darting to the woman who had stopped and watched them with her mouth agape.

"Oh, she is. Just seems to be in charge of making sure everyone's plugged in. Whether you want to be or not. We should go get a seat."

Ursula nodded, but pulled her lip between her teeth. "Do you think...I could sign the sermon for you? I've been practicing."

His eyebrows rose but he nodded. "Sure."

She grinned. She liked his family, it wasn't that. But the idea of sitting with him alone was much more appealing. She slipped her hand into his as they entered the sanctuary and scanned for seats. There was space somewhat near the front. That would be good. Even though her books had arrived and she'd been practicing madly, there were likely to be terms in a sermon she didn't know. If they were closer to the front, maybe Malachi could still read the pastor's lips. Was there a book for specifically church-related signs? She made a mental note to poke around online. At least for the singing they projected the words, so she didn't have to do anything but lose herself in worship.

The sermon was fantastic. The pastor talked about the armor of God from Ephesians six, with a reminder that the devil wanted nothing more than to turn believers away from their calling by getting them to focus on the little details of life instead of what God would have them do. Or by letting them believe lies about themselves. Thus the importance of the armor to protect and defend as a way of daily life. It was too bad she couldn't take notes. She'd have to listen to the podcast later in the week. They had one, didn't they?

Malachi had only looked confused a couple times. When she caught his expression, she jotted a note and made him smile. What had she signed instead? When they stood for the benediction, he took her hand and wove his fingers through hers. Warmth coursed through her.

"Lunch?" He met her gaze as she turned to collect her things.

Ursula nodded. "I'd like that."

"This is Triton." Ursula scooped up the cat and stroked his head before offering him to Malachi.

Malachi pressed his lips together and tentatively ran a hand down the creature's back. He hadn't caught the cat's name the first time he came over. "Triton? Really?"

Ursula shrugged. "I was born after the movie came out, but it was still hilarious in elementary school. So I never wear purple, but otherwise, I can roll with it. I don't look anything like her."

"That's true." He put his hands in his pockets.

Ursula set the cat down. "You said you weren't allergic. So...not a cat fan?"

"Not opposed. Just...not familiar."

Hmm. Well, Triton was a love. If any cat was going to warm someone up and make them a cat person, it was him. "Can I get you anything?"

"I'm good, thanks."

"Okay." She sighed. Lunch at the Sunrise Cafe after church had been great. Now things were stilted and weird. Again. What was she doing wrong?

Malachi closed the distance between them. He took her face in his hands and lowered his mouth to hers.

Ursula closed her eyes and sank into the kiss, her arms winding around his waist.

Malachi eased back, resting his forehead on hers. "I've been waiting to do that since Wednesday."

The corners of her mouth tipped into a smile. "I'm so glad. I was worried. So I..."

He cocked his head to the side. "You?"

Heat crawled up her neck and spread across her cheeks. "Do you like computer games?"

Malachi nodded. "What's not to like?"

"Ever heard of Orion's Quest?"

He nodded again.

She cleared her throat. It shouldn't be this difficult. It's not like it was an alternate life. Not really. Except...it kind of was. She could be fearless and strong in the game. And no one had to know she was dynamite waiting to explode and ruin any relationship she was part of. But it seemed dishonest to keep that part of herself a secret. "I really like that game. I play almost every night. It started out as a way for me and my dad to hang out together. He's not much on email or instant messages. But he'll play a game, you know?"

Malachi smiled. "Sounds like a typical guy."

"I love my dad. When I call home, Mom tends to hog the conversation. And that's fine, I love her, too. But it's nice to have something that's just ours. Anyway...he can't always play when I can, or vice versa, so I started playing more on my own, at first to keep my experience level roughly equal to his so our missions weren't unbalanced and then because I really enjoyed it. And I've made some friends there—which is easier, in many ways, than in person. At least for me. I actually asked one of them, I probably consider him my best friend if we're being honest, if I'd messed things up by kissing you. It's not something I'd normally have done. And anyway, he said not to worry about it. I'm glad he was right. But, um, back to the game." She took a deep breath, her heart hammering in her chest. Her dad was the only other person she'd ever told her screen name to. "If you ever want to play...look me up. I'm Scarlet Fire."

"I know."

All the air seemed to get sucked from her body. She drew her eyebrows together. Her mouth opened and shut several times before she could squeeze out words. "What do you mean?"

"I put it together—almost immediately." Malachi tapped his chest. "I'm MalRen. You...you didn't figure it out?"

She shook her head and couldn't quite figure out how to get it to stop. She blinked as the back of her eyes began to burn. All those conversations...she'd asked about the kiss...oh why couldn't the floor just open and swallow her whole? "Why didn't you say something?"

"I didn't know how to bring it up."

Her churning emotions solidified into a hard, hot ball lodged in her chest. She'd dated a liar once, and that was one time too many. She wasn't going back down that road. Not even for the first man in a long time she'd thought she could love. "That's two things you've lied about and tried to hide. Being deaf and the game. I think maybe you should go. Your website will be live tomorrow. It's probably best if you find someone else to continue with maintenance and updates."

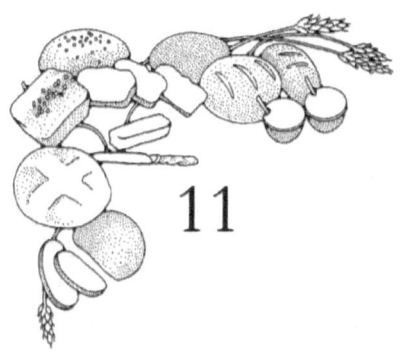

# 11

"You're back a lot sooner than I thought you'd be." Micah hit the mute button on the TV and frowned. "Everything okay?"

Malachi shook his head and kept walking.

Micah appeared in front of him and put a hand on his chest. "Whoa. Dude. What's going on?"

Malachi signed, not trusting his voice. What did a breaking heart sound like? "She dumped me."

"Seriously? What for?"

"I don't want to talk about it." Malachi's hands flashed and he jerked away from his brother. Couldn't people just leave him alone? Everyone had pushed and pushed at him—go make friends, get involved, people don't think you're the dumb deaf guy. Sure. Whatever. Look how well *that* had turned out. He trudged up the stairs and went straight to his room, locking the door behind him before flopping face-first onto the bed.

Now what? He wasn't logging on to the game. That much was certain. Even though his new drive was long past ready and there were missions in the far reaches that promised lucrative bonuses and exploration points. It didn't matter anymore. He'd quit playing solely for fun more than a year ago. It had all been about Scarlet Fire. She was the first person outside his family in...forever...who got him. Or so it had seemed.

Was it another case of missing nuances in people's conversation because he couldn't hear their tone? Sarcasm was often lost on him, but did it go deeper than that? After all, he'd chatted with Ursula via text. How had he still missed her tone? He pounded his fist into the bed. He tried so hard not to blame God. But seriously, wasn't enough enough? He was deaf. The last memories he had of hearing his parents were from when he was a small child. Sure, he had memories of signing with them. But it wasn't the same. He was stuck between two worlds and didn't fit in either one.

He'd tried for the longest time to fit into the hearing world. His family helped. They never—not even once—made his loss of hearing an issue. They'd taken it in stride and signing had become the new normal in their family. To the point that Micah, and possibly the others, but he knew about Micah for sure, had signed while visiting friends even though Malachi hadn't been with them. But outside his family he'd been somewhere on the line between freak and novelty—an object of ridicule or curiosity.

He didn't want to be an object. He just wanted to be Malachi.

So he'd gone to Gallaudet for college and, ironically, had found the reverse of the situation. He did have memories of hearing. And he wasn't willing to cloister himself fully into the deaf community. Though he understood the draw, it didn't sit well with him to exclude the few hearing friends and family members he had. The hearing world wanted him to see his deafness as a disability. The deaf world considered it a benefit. His heart landed somewhere in between.

In the end, he'd withdrawn from both, with the exception of his family. Until now.

Malachi sighed and rolled over onto his back, staring up at the ceiling.

Ursula was half-wrong. He'd never lied about being deaf. Nor had he tried to hide it from her. Everyone in Arcadia Valley—at least everyone he'd run into—had already known, so he'd assumed. And okay, sure, spell out assume. But he wasn't in the habit of saying, "Hi, I'm Malachi, and I'm deaf." He'd had people who didn't believe him in the past. Ruth said it was because he didn't sound deaf when he spoke unless you were really listening for it. But he didn't deny it when someone asked. Why would he?

He hadn't really lied about the game, either. Although you could make—and win—a case for a lie of omission on that one, so it wasn't a point he'd argue. He should've said something to her. Asked. Hinted around. Something. Maybe there'd been a small part of him that enjoyed having that leg up. And if that was the case, it painted a less-than-flattering picture of his character. Did it matter that it wasn't his *intention* to lie?

Probably not.

It was all moot now, anyway. She'd told him to leave. Fired the bakery as a client. It really didn't get much more final than that. He scrubbed a hand over his face. The bakery website was the biggest casualty in all this. She said it was ready, but still, there were bound to be tweaks and updates as they used it for the first several months. It'd be better—easier, certainly—if she'd keep on, at least for a little while.

Maybe Ruth could talk her into it.

Malachi pushed himself off the bed. He opened the door and peeked out a crack. Maybe his brothers really were leaving him alone. He needed a hot shower and then...well, then he'd crawl in bed and stare at nothing until either he fell asleep or it was morning.

He was banking on the latter.

"You're in early." Jonah looked up from kneading a large lump of dough. Micah was busy scooping batter into muffin pans.

Malachi nodded and headed for the office. It wasn't quite six a.m., but he'd meant to get the first newsletter scheduled so it would be delivered and available to their customers first thing. If there was any chance of making that happen, he had to work fast.

Jonah was at his side as Malachi pulled out the desk chair. Was his brother following him? "What?"

"You okay?"

Malachi shook his head. "I will be. Just...leave it. Okay?"

Jonah held his gaze for the space of a few heartbeats before nodding. "Muffins this week are the oat-applesauce-hazelnut. We also have zucchini. Cookies are chocolate chip and oatmeal chocolate chip, special bread is sun-dried tomato. Limited quantities on that last one 'cause it doesn't keep well at all and I'm only making up what gets ordered and a loaf or two each day extra. Won't have any today until almost closing since I'll be waiting to hear from you about orders."

Malachi scribbled down the list and offered it to Jonah to double-check.

"Yep. Holler if you need anything else."

"Get me a photo of the muffins and cookies, would you? If you have some ready?"

"I can do that. Check your email." Jonah patted Malachi on the back and went back into the kitchen.

Malachi closed the door. If Jonah was asking, Micah was concerned and had nagged him into coming to talk to Malachi. Jonah was the second-to-biggest guns when it came to trying to get a sibling to open up. Brushing Jonah off was a risk...but Ruth wouldn't be able to come out until lunch. At the earliest. Maybe by then he'd feel like talking.

For now...he opened the newsletter service and navigated through their clunky design interface. It was time to get this CSB moving forward. And focus on something he could control. He'd set up the header last week—a picture that, if he was honest, came out better than he'd anticipated. Loaves of bread speared out of a basket on top of the bakery display case, more lined the shelves. There were even muffins on display. No cookies. But nothing was perfect. Micah sat in his usual spot by the cash register and Jonah was peeking out the door. It told the story well enough.

His email indicator flashed. Malachi switched to that and considered the photos Jonah sent. They were good—almost artistic. They'd work. He downloaded them to the desktop and went to work with a breezy introduction, a reminder of the perks of local or fair-trade organic ingredients, their new hours, the Saturday farmers market, Wednesday afternoon Twin Falls delivery times, and then outlined the week's specials. He directed them to the website for special orders and quickly switched over to see that the page he needed was, in fact, fully operational. It was. At least Ursula wasn't one of those people who would take out a personal issue on a professional connection.

He hadn't really believed she would. But the doubt had niggled at him.

The email was missing...something. A recipe? But that would send people off to their own kitchens rather than to the bakery. Unless it was for something to go along with the bread? Or maybe a recipe that used it? But who needed a recipe for a sandwich? He smiled and began to type. Corban might be annoyed, but a spotlight on the farmer who provided so many of their staple ingredients, between the wheat and zucchini, seemed like a reasonable addition. Besides, he and Ruth were getting married. He was practically part of the family already.

After another read-through and a few minor tweaks, it was ready to go. Malachi took a deep breath and clicked send just after seven a.m. That should be close enough to first thing to still let people make their choices for any special orders. And if not, well, he'd get it set up to deliver at something like two in the morning next week. For now, the deed was done. He sniffed. And so, apparently, was another batch of muffins. His stomach rumbled. He hadn't made breakfast before heading in. Since he'd told both of his brothers to leave him be, maybe they'd let him snag a muffin without pressing for details. Of course, if they did, it probably meant they'd already roped in Ruth.

Malachi sighed. Either way, he needed something to eat.

"Let's go for a walk." Ruth held out her hand and waited until Malachi took it, then tugged him to his feet.

"Figured you'd show up today." Malachi signed. He was done talking. If people didn't want to learn how to communicate with him, they could just leave him be.

Ruth quirked an eyebrow at him and responded in kind. "Eat lunch yet?"

He shook his head. He'd had three muffins after sending the newsletter and had been tempted to go for a fourth, but Jonah's pointed look had sent him back into the office. On the positive side, people were, so far, responsive to the email. He'd passed on the special orders as they came in, although they were going to need to work out something for planning to match special orders with usual pick up or delivery days. Malachi had been playing with the database all morning, trying to get it to print a report that made sense.

"Good. I packed something for us. Founders Park?"

He shrugged. "Sure."

"Walk or drive?"

Malachi shrugged again.

Ruth frowned. "I'll drive. Let's go."

Malachi stared out the window as she drove the few blocks to the park. They could've walked. It was a nice, if warm, summer day. But someone would've had to carry the cooler Ruth had wedged in the back seat, and given the size of the thing, it was probably heavy. And she wouldn't have been the one toting it.

Ruth pulled into a parking spot and touched his arm. "Grab the lunch, would you?"

Exactly. He sighed and pushed open the door, got out, and closed it. Why did she bring a cooler this size? Was it the only one she had? If that was the case, he knew what he was getting her for her birthday. Or Christmas. Or as a wedding gift. He'd take whatever came first. He grunted as he hefted the thing and followed behind Ruth as she scouted out the perfect spot under a tree.

Malachi set down the cooler and pried up the lid. A blanket sat on top. He took it out and shook it, letting it fall to the ground. He tugged the corners until it was basically straight and then sat.

"Not going to help?" Ruth smirked and sat next to the food. She reached in and unloaded several small containers of food, as well as two plates and some silverware.

Malachi let out a breath. He'd been half-afraid this was some kind of ambush and that Ruth had invited Ursula to join them. Or, worse, that she'd leave him here when Ursula showed up. If she even would. And that was a big, big *if.* The woman was steamed.

"Grab what's near you, load up your plate, and spill it."

In spite of himself, he smiled. "You have a way with words."

"It's a gift." Ruth reached across and squeezed his hand. "Micah and Jonah are worried about you. Which means I am, too. What happened?"

The whole story came pouring out, including some of his thoughts from last night. When he finished, he dropped his hands in his lap and looked down at the plate in front of him, his appetite gone.

"Wow." Ruth forked up a bite of pasta salad and nudged his plate closer to him.

Malachi shook his head.

She tapped his leg and waited 'til he looked up. "You need to eat, Mal."

"Fine." He picked up a pickle spear and bit into it, offering her an overly bright smile as he chewed.

"Better. What are you going to do?"

"Nothing. There's nothing *to* do."

Ruth frowned. "You're not going to fight for her?"

"Why? She made herself very clear. I think, at this point, I need to just leave it be and see if Jonah or Micah can convince her to keep us as a client. Maybe if they promise she won't have to deal with me, she'll agree."

"Malachi." Ruth touched his leg.

Hot tears burned the back of his eyes but he had no intention of letting them fall. He didn't need any random passers-by labeling him the crybaby deaf guy. Bad enough that he was Arcadia Valley's newest oddity. "You don't understand."

"I think, maybe, I do. It's hard to move somewhere new. To be the person that everyone knows doesn't belong. I don't know what it's like to be different on top of that, true. But Mal, the people here have been so welcoming. You know they're glad you're here, right?"

Did he? Grace Fellowship was a warm, welcoming church. But they still stared when Ruth signed the sermon for him. Some of the older members of the congregation frowned. Probably because it distracted them to have her hands moving. But he couldn't help that. It was either have the sermon interpreted or go without. And if he was going without, he'd just stay home. Maybe that was the better solution. Despite what Ruth said, it was doubtful anyone would notice. "I don't know. I don't think there's any way to know unless I leave."

"No!" Ruth looked stricken. She grabbed his hand, clutching so hard it hurt. "You can't leave. Where would you go? Not over something like this. Please."

Malachi pried his fingers out of Ruth's grasp and picked up his plate. He poked the pasta salad. She'd put olives in it. Ruth didn't, as a rule, care for olives in her pasta salad. But she knew they were his favorite. He looked more closely at the food on the blanket. They were all his favorites. His shoulders slumped and he set the food down so he could sign. "I'm not. I just wish I could. But since you wouldn't come with me, there's no point. You, Micah, and Jonah are all that matter."

"And Ursula?"

"I thought—hoped—she could matter too. I was wrong. I'll be okay." But he wouldn't. Not really. Scarlet Fire had been his ideal woman for too long. To meet her and realize that the reality was even better than the online persona and then have them both ripped away? How did he recover from that? And what would be the point? If Ursula, who understood him better than anyone who wasn't one of his siblings, could kick him out of her life so easily, no one else was going to want to keep him. He was too flawed. Damaged. Unlovable.

Ruth bit her lip. He could see her struggling not to unleash a litany of why that wasn't good enough. After a minute she nodded. "We'll leave it there for now. I love you. You know that, right?"

Malachi nodded. "Same goes."

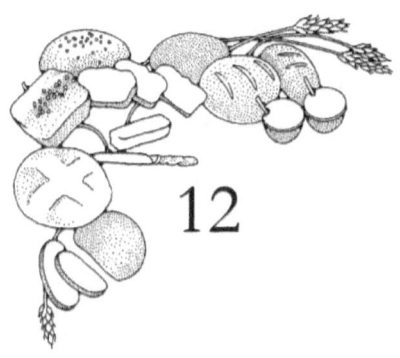

# 12

Ursula stepped out of the airport doors and was slapped back by the wall of hot, humid air that embodied mid-August in South Carolina. Dragging her roller bag behind her, she crossed the street to the rental car lot and walked down the aisle, looking for the number that matched her key. She could've called her parents. They would've picked her up if she'd let them know she was coming, but she hadn't been convinced she was. She'd stayed home, brooding, on Monday and most of yesterday. Then she'd gone online and bought a ticket home.

There it was. She clicked the key fob to unlock the doors and pop the trunk. After hefting in her bag and settling her laptop case next to it, she got in and took a deep breath. The roads were basically empty. Not a surprise for the middle of the day on Wednesday. Would her parents even be home? They were retired, but they lived an active, full life. Had Dad dragged Mom off on a road trip to find more forgotten cemeteries? Surely he would've mentioned that when she'd played with him online the last two days. Malachi had never logged in. Not that she had been watching for him. Not really. It had been...idle curiosity. At best.

Oh, who was she kidding? Her heart ached from the loss of him.

Still. It didn't matter. She'd asked him to go, rightfully. It was good he was respecting her wishes and leaving her alone. She didn't have room in her life for a liar. Ursula shut down the quiet whispers in the back of her mind that wanted to argue about whether or not he'd really lied. Omission counted. She swallowed the lump forming in her throat. She was done crying over Malachi Baxter.

Columbia was one of those cities where it seemed like nothing ever changed. And yet, there were differences from the last time she'd been home. New houses going in, shopping centers that changed colors and stores. Just enough to prove life moved on, no matter where she lived. She pulled off the highway at the north end of town and wound around to the big subdivision where her parents had moved six years ago, downsizing to a more reasonably sized home for the retirement years. The single-story rambler had three bedrooms and vaulted ceilings in the master and living rooms. Her mother alternated between loving and hating them, depending on how well the fans worked to keep the air moving. Ursula pulled her rental up to the curb in front of the house and got out. She'd leave her bags for now.

Dad had planted brightly colored flowers in the beds that lined the walk to the door. She smiled. Mom probably argued for some kind of green groundcover.

Low maintenance and unobtrusive. But Dad liked to putter in the garden when it wasn't hotter than surface of the sun outside, and so Mom tended to let him have his way. Mom certainly wasn't going to be digging in the garden anytime soon.

Ursula pushed the doorbell.

"Can you get that? I'm up to my elbows in soapy water."

Ursula smiled. Her mom never wanted to answer the door. Dad's grumble wasn't as clear, but she heard a chair roll on the wood floor and footsteps stomp toward the door.

"Hi, Dad."

"Urs? Hey there, baby." Her father flung open the door and pulled her into his arms, squeezing her hard. "Did we know you were coming? You mother says I'm getting forgetful. Maybe I am. I'll have to start taking that gecko extract she keeps trying to force on me."

Ursula chuckled. "Ginkgo, Dad? And no, you didn't know I was coming. *I* didn't know I was coming until last night."

He studied her face. "What's wrong, honey?"

Her eyes filled and she shook her head. "Can we talk about it later, maybe?"

"Of course. Come on, your mother's going to be so thrilled you're here. Is that your car? You know we would've come to get you."

"Where's the fun in that?" She turned the corner to the kitchen and cleared her throat. "Surprise."

Her mother dropped the pan she was scrubbing and hurried over, leaving a trail of sudsy water on the floor. "Ursula! Oh, you're here. What on earth...oh, fiddlesticks."

Laughing, Ursula's mom grabbed the towel off the kitchen island and dried her arms before dragging Ursula into another tight hug. "Did you and your father plan this?"

Dad held up his hands. "I didn't know she was coming either."

"What happened?" Her mother's piercing gaze locked onto Ursula's.

"I just...needed to come home for a bit. I'm headed back on Saturday." She cleared her throat. The round trip ticket had been cheaper. Even if she wasn't positive heading back to Arcadia Valley was the right move. She'd have to go back to pack up and get Triton anyway, if it came to that.

"Well. You know you're always welcome. Let me go check on the guest room. I think it might need new sheets on the bed. I can't think the last time it was used, so they're probably full of dust. Did you eat lunch?"

"Mom. It's okay. Finish what you were doing. I know how to change a bed. I...maybe I could lie down for a little bit?"

Her parents exchanged a glance.

Dad held out his hand. "Gimme your keys, I'll go get your bags."

"I'll help you with the sheets. You know it's always easier with two people." Her mother smiled and slid an arm around her shoulders. "Then you take a little rest. It's nearly time for my own afternoon siesta."

Ursula leaned her head on her mother's shoulder. "Thanks, Mom."

"Anytime, baby. Anytime."

Ursula lay on her side tucked under the quilt her grandma had made and stared at the closed door of her parents' guest room. Mom and Dad were talking about her in voices that they clearly thought were whispers. It should be amusing. Maybe in a few days it would be. She hadn't meant to upset them—worry them—by coming home. She'd just needed to be there. Even if it wasn't the house she'd grown up in, it was filled with familiar things. With them.

She should get up, wash her face, and go out there. Explain. Her insides tightened. What if they disagreed with her? If she was honest, she came home because she wanted—needed—them to tell her that she wasn't that bad. That what she'd done was reasonable. That there wasn't something so inordinately flawed in her that Malachi's behavior was okay. Justified, even. Because she was struggling to believe any of that. This kept happening time after time. So-called friend after so-called friend. And she was the only common denominator.

Forcing her muscles to cooperate, Ursula pushed back the quilt and stood. She stretched her arms above her head, working out the stiffness from the plane and nap, before padding to the door and pulling it open. Dad had fixed the squeaking hinge since she'd last been there. She managed a slight smile and aimed for the hall bathroom. The shower called to her, but there'd be time for that later. She splashed water on her face and blotted it dry with a hand towel, then scrutinized her reflection.

The dark circles under her eyes were still there, but she looked a little less pale, a tad less hollow. She pulled the rubber band out of her hair, ran her fingers through it, and then gathered it back into a ponytail. She didn't look great, but it would have to do.

"Oh, good. You're up. I was just coming to check on you." Mom smiled and pulled Ursula into another hug. "Want some cocoa?"

"Cocoa? It's nine hundred degrees outside, Mom."

"It's only ninety-six. And with the new-fangled central air we have, it's a pleasant seventy-six in the living room." Mom shook her head. "Honestly. Just say no. Iced tea?"

Ursula's mouth watered. Her mother's sweet tea was worth a visit on its own merits. The key was adding the sugar while the tea was hot so it got super-saturated. And yet...it never tasted as good in Arcadia Valley. "Yes, please."

"Come on in and have a seat in the living room and I'll bring it out."

"You don't..." Ursula watched her mother hurry off and shrugged. Fine. She didn't get waited on all that often, even when she visited. Dad was in the recliner with his feet up. His glasses were perched on the tip of his nose while he read the latest spy thriller he'd borrowed from the library. "Any good?"

He tucked a bookmark in and set the book aside. "It's okay. Already figured out who's behind the plot, so it's just a matter of watching it play out. A little more predictable than I like. But it's set in London, and that at least makes the scenery interesting. Feeling a little better?"

"Yeah, thanks. Should I have called first to make sure it was okay to come?" Ursula tucked her feet under her and tugged a blanket off the back of the couch, tossing it over her legs. Between the A/C and the ceiling fan, it was a little cool.

"What kind of question is that? Honestly." Her mom handed her a glass of iced tea and set a plate of cookies on the coffee table in front of her. "You're welcome here any time. With no notice at all. Especially when you're hurting. Won't you tell us what happened?"

Ursula took a long drink, the sweetness on her tongue relaxing. "I told you, a little, about Malachi. Right?"

Her parents nodded.

She walked them through the situation. From finding out he was deaf—something apparently everyone but she knew—to the whole Orion's Quest issue.

"So he just left? Without saying anything in his defense?" Dad frowned, shaking his head.

"Now, Jim, what was the boy supposed to do? Ursula asked him to go, and he did. As he should. You wouldn't like someone who tried to stay, either." Mom sighed. "He hasn't said anything since, though? No texts or emails?"

Ursula shook her head.

"See?" Her dad shot a triumphant look at her mom. "He's not worth your time, baby. You'll find someone who'll fight for you. Just hang in there."

"I don't want someone who's going to fight for me, Dad. There's something *wrong* with me. Honestly, at this point I'm just glad it happened early on, before we were serious about each other. Better to realize now that he already saw whatever it is about me that poisons every relationship."

"What nonsense is this?" Her mother bristled. "Ursula Marie Franks, explain yourself."

She hunched her shoulders. Why was it that even at the ripe old age of twenty-seven, when Mom trotted out her full name, her insides quivered? Her tongue darted between her lips. "Look at history, Mom. Go back to middle school. Friend after so-called friend has done something along these lines. Remember Laura? Genny? What about Brian or Mark or even Jamal? I know you think it's on them. But seriously? I'm the only thing in common with the situation. There has to be something about me that's unlovable long-term, as a friend or in a romantic sense. Better to find out now with Malachi, don't you think? And really, having this happen again...it solidifies that my decision not to put myself out there was the right one. Why give people the chance to remind me how worthless I am?" A tear slipped down her cheek. Ursula brushed it away and stood, her stomach churning.

"I'm going back to my room. Don't feel like you have to hold dinner."

Ursula ran down the hall, closed the door behind her, and flung herself on the bed before heaving sobs wracked her body. Why did God bother to make her if she was so repugnant to everyone around her that they had to lie about or to her? It wasn't as if she had some grand purpose. She wasn't in the mission field, bringing people to Jesus. She wasn't a doctor who saved lives. She was one of a zillion freelance web designers trying to scratch out a living for herself doing something she enjoyed. Whoopee. Was it even fair to her clients to work with them if she was the horrible person the people she thought were friends made her out to be? No, she did darn good work. That was the one thing no one could fault her on.

She could have loved Malachi.

The thought was unbidden. And sobering. Gingerly, she turned it over in her head. Even the first day they'd met in person, when he'd faded into the background after his family came, she'd been drawn to him. Heck, she'd been curious enough to seek him out. She hadn't needed to in order to do her job. It had felt like she'd known him for a while, which, she supposed, was true. She just hadn't realized it. Had he known from the start and planned to use it somehow for...what? No. That was ridiculous even to her. But when he figured it out, he should've said something. How hard was it to say, "Hey, I play this online game, do you?"

There was a quiet tap at the door.

Sighing, she sat up and dragged Grandma's quilt over her legs. "Come in."

"Hi." Dad stood in the doorway, his hands in his pockets. "Can I sit?"

"Of course. I'm sorry, Daddy."

He shook his head and lowered himself to the edge of the bed. "Nothing to be sorry about. Except, maybe, for how critical you are of my daughter."

She blinked. "But, Dad..."

He held up a hand. "Ursula, I won't deny you've been treated badly by a lot of people in your life. I'm not sure I'm ready to lump this boy in with them, mind you, as it seems like he might've had some hurts himself that made it hard for him to behave exactly the way you wanted."

He was defending Malachi? Her mouth opened to protest.

Dad shook his head. "Not finished. I'm not excusing him, yet. But I do think he deserves a chance to tell you his side of things. If it was me, I would've taken that chance before I let you kick me out. But he's not me. And when I look at what he did, I have to figure he's pretty used to getting kicked around, too, so he didn't see the point in trying to fight."

"Maybe." It was something to think about. "But..."

"The bigger issue, honey, is inside you."

Her heart sank and her shoulders fell. She drew her knees to her chest and curled her arms around them. "I know."

"I don't think you do. You're convinced that because people have treated you badly you're somehow to blame. That you're broken. I disagree. Sure, you've had your share—maybe more than your share—of friend drama. Seems to me that's just part of life. It's what you do with it that matters. You can, of course, hole yourself up in that pretty little bungalow in Arcadia Valley and only interact with people online. Or you can let go of the notion that we're entitled to have people treat us the way we'd like."

She couldn't keep the sullen out of her tone. "'Cause there's nothing in the Bible about that."

Her dad smiled. "Didn't say that. Ideally, yes, everyone would believe in Jesus and strive to love Him with their heart, soul and mind. And then, following on that—since it's necessary for the second to work—they'd love their neighbors as themselves. Problem is, not everyone does believe in Jesus, and even Christians sometimes get so caught up in the idea of loving others that they forget step one, loving God wholeheartedly. And if we're trying to love others on our own power, we're going to fail. Badly."

"I don't really see what this has to do with Malachi."

"It doesn't, not directly. I got a little sidetracked. But the point is there. Honey, you're holding on to past hurts, and it's impacting your ability to love God and others—in a generic sense and, in the case of this boy, in a romantic one. I'll ask this one question and go: were you looking for opportunities for him to let you down or

were you focused on the possibility that he might not?"
He patted her knee and stood, dropping a kiss on the top
of her head. "Don't stay in here too long. Your mother's
making your favorite for dinner."

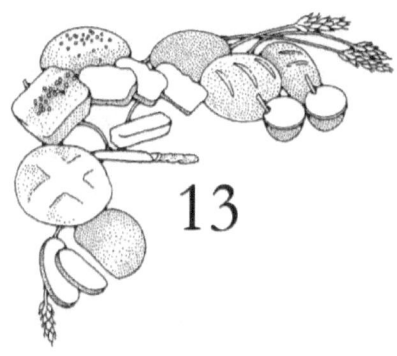

# 13

Ruth hadn't left it alone. Neither had his brothers. Oh, they were subtle, but by Friday, Malachi was rethinking...a lot of different things. Like maybe he was overly sensitive about being deaf. That stung. He'd tried so hard not to be someone who looked for slights in every conversation. And he'd ended up there anyway.

He owed Ursula an apology.

When he finished with the morning office tasks at the bakery, he squared his shoulders and went out to the display case. There were still muffins—the oat and nut was a big hit. They were starting to get a trickle of people coming in to grab a muffin or a cookie on the way in to work and randomly throughout the day as a treat. Enough that Malachi had spent some time pricing basic coffee equipment. They could set up a self-serve station and it wouldn't add much work for whoever was manning the register. It wouldn't be fancy, just drip—maybe have decaf as an option as well—but it was something to bring up at the next meeting. Whenever that ended up happening.

The zucchini muffins hadn't been quite the sellers the oat-nut were. But then, if what Corban said was true, everyone was swimming in their own zucchini already. Hopefully the folks at the food bank were enjoying them. Mid-week, Jonah had started putting a cream cheese filling in the center. That had helped a little. But only a little.

Malachi popped up one of the bakery boxes he'd talked his brothers into and loaded it with six muffins. "Ring these up, would you?"

Micah looked surprised but nodded. "You do know we don't have to pay, right?"

He shrugged and dug some bills out of his wallet. "Feels like I'm better off paying for a peace offering."

"Atta boy." Micah punched Malachi's shoulder. "You don't think flowers are a better choice?"

Were they? He didn't really want to drive all the way down to Blossoms by the Akers. And with them so close, grocery store flowers weren't going to cut it. He frowned and shook his head. "I'm going with muffins. If it's wrong, well, so be it."

"Fair enough. I'll be praying."

Malachi gave a slight smile. He wasn't looking for miracles. Right now, he'd be content if she agreed to keep their website business. There were two or three little tweaks that needed to be made and he was hesitant to try and do it himself. He would, if push came to shove, but...hopefully it wouldn't. It'd probably only take Ursula five minutes. If Malachi tried, they were talking hours.

He stepped out into the heat and tilted his face to the sun. The office had no window. He needed to do better about getting out of the cave. For all his protests about not needing people in his life, he did. His family was enough. They were there for him, which was more than so many people had. He needed to stop taking them for granted. With his online game no longer a possibility, he'd been spending the evening on the main floor with Micah, Jonah, and, when the B&B was busy, Corban. His sister had a keeper there. She needed to hurry up and set a date. Did she realize it was making Corban anxious that she hadn't?

Tucking the bakery box under his arm, he grabbed his phone from his pocket and tapped out a text to Ruth. If she could be blunt with him about his relationships, well, he'd just return the favor. After crossing the major avenue that ran north to south through town, Malachi ambled down the neighborhood street. He waved to the old man out on his porch in a lawn chair. The man waved back. Did Ursula like living in town with a tiny little yard or did she yearn for something more like Corban's farmhouse? He had so many questions...and he needed to focus on step one. Apologize and attempt to reestablish a business relationship. Maybe they could find their way to more after that. But this time, he wasn't skipping steps.

He knocked briskly on her door. The cat—what was his name? Something from that movie...Tintin? Triton—watched him from the window in the living room, the tip of his tail flicking. He frowned and knocked again. Had she seen it was him, somehow, and decided not to answer? Shoulders drooping, he considered the bakery box. He wasn't going to go back with them. But if she wasn't answering...they weren't going to be any good if she left them out in the heat for any appreciable time.

Malachi trudged down the steps and crossed the street. He turned up the walk that led to the old man's house with a brief wave. At the bottom of the steps, he stopped and took a deep breath. He hadn't spoken to anyone since Sunday—he'd only signed—Ursula's accusation that he'd hidden his deafness was a wound that wouldn't close. He held out the bakery box. He'd make this one exception and then go back to being scrupulously pointed about signing. "Would you like some muffins?"

The old man frowned and touched his ear. "What's that?"

Malachi let out a tiny snort. Was the man deaf? There was no evidence of hearing aids, so it seemed unlikely that it was old-age-related hearing loss. Though it could just be he didn't wear the aids. Still, worth a shot. This time he signed. "Would you like some muffins?"

The man beamed, his whole face transforming as he nodded and signed in response. "Certainly. You sign well."

Malachi set the box on the man's lap. "I've been deaf since I was five. I'm Malachi Baxter."

"Amos Greenway. Pleasure to meet you." He lifted the lid of the box and grinned. "Will you sit and have a muffin?"

Malachi considered. He had work he could be doing. But it wasn't pressing. He nodded. "I'd like that."

Amos pointed to a matching lawn chair that was folded by the front door. "Pull up a chair and sit for a spell. I've seen you a few times with the young lady across the way. You courtin'?"

Malachi shook his head and finally got the rusty chair unfolded. "Thought things might go that way, but no. These were to try and at least get her to keep doing some work at the bakery."

Amos nodded. It was a contemplative gesture Malachi recognized. With the subtle tremor age often lent to limbs, Amos took a muffin from the box and offered the container to Malachi. Malachi plucked a zucchini muffin for himself. Might as well leave the best sellers for the old man.

"Tell me about your bakery." Amos bit into the muffin and smiled. "These remind me of when my Alma was alive."

So Malachi related the story of how Ruth inherited the Fairview B&B and then he and his brothers came to Arcadia Valley, culminating in the start of A Slice of Heaven. "And when we decided we needed a website, I ended up meeting Ursula. And then I ruined it."

"Women are a mystery, it's true." Amos patted Malachi's shoulder. "And now I'm eating your peace offering."

"She didn't answer the door. They wouldn't keep in the heat. This is better all-around." Malachi leaned back in the chair and stared out across the neighborhood. He could see why Amos sat out here.

"It's a good block. Nice to see young people moving in now that Main Street's bustling. Seems like for a while the folks in Twin Falls forgot we were more than just farmers. Then we seemed to forget ourselves. But now, we've got good businesses, thriving churches, and some artists. Folks who maybe don't want the town life can live here and work there and have the best of both worlds. It's a lot like it was when Alma and I moved out here, back when Stargil Enterprises was just starting up."

"You worked in the factory?"

Amos nodded. "'Till it cost me my ears. Got a decent settlement out of it. We thought about moving, but this is home. Even if it took folks a while to adjust to me needing to have Alma around to interpret for me all the time. Learned to sign okay, but lip reading...never could catch on to that reliably."

Malachi swallowed. Would Amos understand? "You didn't feel...I don't know...like a freak? Or an object of pity?"

"Oh maybe. Fact is, I was older so maybe my experience isn't completely the same. But it wore off, by and large. Though there's still one woman who talks at me like I'm an idiot when she comes by." Amos grinned and shrugged. "Since she looks like an idiot, not me, I just ignore it."

Malachi laughed. Maybe that was the right attitude. In D.C., he'd hardly given a thought to his impairment. Meeting someone new hadn't filled him with dread like it did here. Had he just become too sensitive with the move? It was something to consider. "Are you still keeping the yard yourself?"

Amos shook his head. "Alma and I attended Arcadia Valley Community Church for so many years they still come out and do the grass in the summer and shovel me out in the winter. They show up with food now and then as well, though since I putter around well enough in the kitchen I think that's more to be sociable. They're good people. You going to church?"

"Yes sir. Grace Fellowship, for now, though maybe I ought to try the other, seeing as how I end up in my brothers' pockets all day every day. Getting away on Sundays might be just what I need."

"They don't have an interpreter. Alma always signed for me. So if you can read lips, sit up front and you'll probably be fine. Otherwise, you might need to stick with family. But they're a good bunch."

Malachi nodded. He could probably read lips well enough. Ruth would be annoyed, maybe even hurt. And that wasn't what he was trying to do. Still, it was worth thinking about. He pulled out his phone to check the time. "I should head back. It was nice to chat with you. Would you mind if I stopped by again?"

"I hope you will. If you want to put your number in my phone, I can text you if I see your young lady." Amos pulled a cell phone from the breast pocket of his shirt. "I use it to text my grandkids. Texting...best thing in the world for people like us."

Malachi grinned and programmed his number in then sent himself a text. "It really is."

Malachi pushed open the door and stepped into the warmth of the B&B's kitchen. His brothers were heading to bed early. They had to get up in time to bake for the farmers market in the morning, which made for pretty dull Friday nights as far as Malachi was concerned. They kept threatening to try and teach him to bake so he could take a rotation. He'd give it a shot if they insisted, but he couldn't hear the timers and they didn't have the kitchen set up to be adaptive. Which was a lame excuse. He could use his phone as timer and it would flash at him. But his mother had declared him basically hopeless in the kitchen and Mom would've known. How had they forgotten?

He pulled open the fridge and rooted through the containers of leftovers. Aha. There was the lasagna Ruth had mentioned. His mouth watered as he peeled up one corner and sniffed. A minute or two in the microwave and—someone tapped his shoulder. He jumped and turned.

Ruth grinned. "Sneaking dinner?"

He set the container down so he could sign. "That okay? You said there was lasagna."

"It's fine." She cocked her head to the side. "You'll stay and hang out? Emerson and Pam are coming by, with their boys, for dessert later. So it's not like you'd be a third wheel."

Fifth wheel, though. He put the container in to cook. But without his game, what other option did he have? Maybe he should consider one of the multitude of other online role-playing games. He could start fresh and choose a character name like DeafMalachi. Then there'd never be any confusion. "We'll see."

Ruth nudged him out of the way and reached for the microwave door. She pulled out the container and set it on the counter. She reached into a cupboard and grabbed a plate.

"I can do that." Malachi reached for the plate.

She shook her head. "I don't get to do this as much now that you three live over with Corban. And I don't blame you, from everything Micah and Jonah have said, it's a much better arrangement. But I miss you."

He smiled.

Ruth looked up at him through her eyelashes. "You're not going to leave, are you Mal?"

He shook his head. He'd never been serious about that.

She beamed. "I'm so glad. Corban mentioned you took some muffins to Ursula this morning?"

He frowned. How would Corban have heard about that?

"I think he bumped into Jonah before coming over. And while your brother might be willing to leave it alone and not pry, I'm not. Sit down. You can tell me while you eat." Ruth set the plate at the kitchen table and pulled out a chair.

Malachi sat and forked up a bite of the pasta. No one made lasagna like his sister. Mom had taught her grandma's recipe when Ruth was only eight. She made the tomato sauce from scratch, and that was probably a big portion of what made it so good. He set down the fork. "Nothing to tell. She wasn't home."

"You left the muffins?"

He shook his head and offered a tiny smile.

Ruth smacked the table. "Don't be a jerk, Mal. Tell me what happened. I know the muffins didn't go back to the bakery with you and, given that you're sitting here eating dinner, I don't think you ate all six of them by yourself to save the embarrassment of bringing them back."

"I gave them to her neighbor. We had a good chat. I went back to work. Okay?" He'd forgotten the pushy, had-to-know-everything, side of Ruth. She didn't let it out very often, which was a good thing.

"That wasn't so hard, was it?" Her expression softened. "I'm sorry she didn't answer. Do you think she was home?"

He shrugged. "No way to know. Amos is going to text me if he sees her."

"Amos?"

"Her neighbor. I'm going to sign him up for the CSB, on me. He's gotta be ninety four if he's a day. He says the folks at his church take good care of him, but a loaf of fresh, local bread? Why would he turn that down?

He liked the muffins." Malachi scraped the last bites of lasagna off his plate and scooted back in his chair. "Have I been moping since I moved here?"

Ruth's eyebrows shot up. "Moping? No. But...I do think this transition has been hardest on you."

He nodded. "I'm sorry."

She reached across the table and covered his hand with her own. "You don't need to be. I know this is difficult. And Ursula didn't make it any easier. You liked her."

It wasn't a question, but he nodded anyway. Somehow it was easier to admit it than to try and brush it off.

"Well, don't give up, okay? People have miscommunications all the time."

Malachi shook his head. This was more than a misunderstanding. "You've always been an optimist."

Ruth laughed. "That's not a word I'd ever use to describe myself."

"Hopeless romantic then?"

"Maybe. At least try to work it out with her? I liked her."

"I'll try." Malachi stood and carried his plate to the sink. "I think I'm going to go home. Appreciate dinner. Will you be by the farmers market tomorrow?"

"Yeah. Corban wanted me to help at his booth. You going to be there?"

He shrugged. "Least I can do is man the stall. Micah and Jonah have to get up and bake. They deserve to go home and nap afterward."

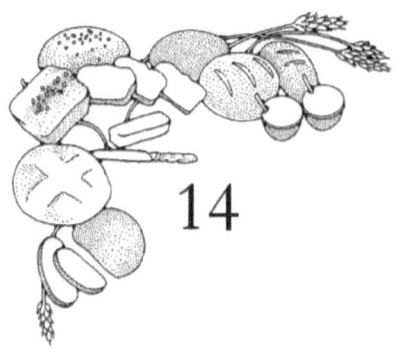

# 14

Ursula scooped up Triton and rubbed his ears. "Did you miss me?"

His purr rumbled in his chest and he let out a *prrrow.*

"Well, I missed you. Anything to tell me about?" She set him down in front of his dish. She reached for one of the few cans of food she kept for special treats and opened it before scooping half into a bowl, noting that his automatic feeder still had plenty of dry food in it. He made a contented noise before settling on his haunches to eat. "I'm glad it was uneventful. I had a good visit with Mom and Dad. They might actually come and see us. I guess I piqued their interest for the first time since I moved here. I wonder just how much Malachi has to do with that."

She shook her head and went to her bedroom, dragging her suitcase with her. Malachi. The conversation with her father still echoed in her head. Had she been waiting for him to let her down? Whether or not she'd been waiting for it, he had. Hadn't he? How long had they been friends online...and never once had he thought to mention he was hearing impaired? Although, they really hadn't shared much personal information, so maybe that made sense. And she'd never asked why he always used chat instead of the in-game voice channels. She'd just assumed...all kinds of things like maybe he didn't have the equipment or there was something wrong with his voice. She'd imagined a stutter or a very high pitch. And then she'd dismissed it from her mind. It wasn't like everyone online used a microphone.

So, fine. Maybe he hadn't kept it as a big secret. He hadn't denied it when she brought it up. But he'd figured out who she was and hadn't said anything, leaving her to broach the embarrassing subject. Wait. Had it been pride behind her anger? Heat flooded her face and she closed her eyes. That was a lowering thought. Oh, what had she done?

Ursula unzipped her rolling bag and grabbed up all her clothes in one big lump. She carried them to the bathroom and dropped them in the hamper then sat on the edge of the tub. She couldn't undo what had happened. But maybe she could figure out a way to fix it. Step one? Reply to the email she'd gotten from Micah— and oh the pangs in her heart that Malachi hadn't been the one to write—asking her to stay on as their web designer until they could find someone new. Well, they didn't need to find someone new, that much was certain. Step two? She didn't have one yet. But something would come to her. It usually did.

Ursula scanned the foyer of Grace Fellowship. There was Jonah. And Ruth and Corban. But where was Malachi? With Micah somewhere? Maybe trying out a small group or hanging back in the sanctuary to talk to the pastor? She wove through the crowd and peeked through the doors into the mostly-empty worship center. No Malachi.

Someone tapped her shoulder. She turned. "Oh. Hi, Ruth."

"Hi. I didn't think we'd see you today."

Heat flooded Ursula's face. She didn't want to apologize to his sister before she talked to him though. "Yeah. I...wasn't sure I'd be here either."

Ruth nodded, a smile playing at the corners of her lips. "Well, it's nice to see you. Have a good Sunday."

"Sure. Thanks." Ursula chewed on her lower lip as Ruth turned. "Wait."

Ruth stopped and faced her again.

"Is Malachi here?"

Ruth smiled and shook her head. "Nope. Not today. Sorry."

She opened her mouth and snapped it shut. She wasn't going to beg. Clearly there was a wall of sibling solidarity going on here. And that was fine. Good, even. "Okay. Thanks."

Ruth cocked her head to the side. "Want to join me for lunch?"

"I...don't you have plans with your fiancé? I don't want to intrude." Ursula's stomach sank. It might be fun to have lunch with a girl friend...not that Ruth was any sort of friend. Yet. And it wasn't as if Ursula was the kind of person who made friends—no, stop. She was done with that line of thinking.

"He's fine. Ever since you and Malachi went to El Corazon, I've been dying to try it. I'm told they have a good brunch buffet on Sunday."

Ursula's mouth watered. "If you're sure...I'd like that a lot."

Ruth grinned. "Absolutely. I'll meet you there?"

"Okay. Thanks, Ruth." Ursula waved and crossed the foyer. Maybe at lunch Ruth would be more forthcoming about Malachi's whereabouts. Or...maybe she should let it rest. She could just send him an email. Or a text. He didn't seem to be playing Orion's Quest anymore. She'd logged in last night and checked. He hadn't been on since the night she kicked him out.

The restaurant was on the way out of town, but it still didn't take long to reach. The parking lot was fuller than she'd anticipated. Although really, who could resist Mexican food? And a brunch buffet to boot. She pulled into a spot and cut the engine. Her stomach jittered. When was the last time she'd sat down to a meal with another woman who hadn't been her mom? Or a business contact? Too long to figure. She blew out a breath. She could do this.

Ursula crossed to the restaurant and pulled open the door. She scanned the tables but didn't see Ruth. She raised two fingers and followed the hostess to a small booth wedged in the back corner. The scent of chorizo and huevos rancheros reached her and her stomach rumbled. It'd be rude to start without her though. A glass of water appeared as the server efficiently moved between tables.

"Hi. You're quick." Ruth hung her purse across the back of her chair and grinned. "They said to just grab a plate and start if we were doing the buffet?"

Ursula nodded and stood. "Definitely the buffet."

She followed behind Ruth, taking a little bit of everything as they slid down the line. All the smells mingled into a tantalizing aroma of spice and meat. And it was all distinctly Mexican. Back at their table, Ruth said a quick grace before Ursula reached for her fork.

"I'm so glad you thought of this place. I don't get down here as much as I should. There's a Mexican restaurant in Columbia, where my parents live, and we go every time I'm home because I'm craving their salsa. But I forget El Corazon is right here." Ursula pushed at the spoonful of beans that was trying to ooze into her rice.

Ruth sipped from her steaming mug, her eyebrows lifting. "Wow. Did you get the hot chocolate?"

Ursula wrinkled her nose. "I've tried it. Not my thing. But I'm glad you're enjoying it."

A man who appeared to be the manager was walking from table to table, asking everyone how they liked the food, whether everything was okay. He was cordial and obviously concerned about the customers, but there was a don't-come-too-close look in his eyes. Ursula recognized it because she'd worn the same expression often enough. And was trying to stop doing it.

"That's Javier Quintana," Ruth whispered after he'd walked away. "Handsome, right? Women love him, but he doesn't date. Supposedly, he never got over his high school sweetheart." And then she looked hard into Ursula's eyes. "So. Do you want to tell me what happened with Malachi?"

Ursula blinked at the abrupt change of subject, her fork halfway to her mouth. With effort, she finished the bite and chewed. He hadn't told his family? She took a long drink of water. "Um. What did he say?"

"That he didn't want to talk about it."

Ursula looked down at her plate, her appetite gone. "Maybe I shouldn't, then. I mean...I don't know...it seems weird."

Ruth sighed. "You're probably right. I just hate not knowing. Because that means not being able to help. And that's...probably exactly what he'd like to avoid. He's a grown man, for all that he's my little brother. I worry about him, though."

"I'm pretty sure he knows you love him." Ursula patted her beans with her fork, concentrating on making intersecting hash marks in their surface.

"Yeah, I know. But the two of you were good together. It bothers me that it seems to be over."

Ursula cleared her throat and raised her eyes to meet Ruth's. "Do you think there's any chance I can fix things?"

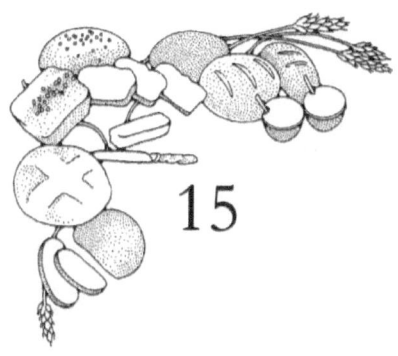

# 15

Malachi offered Amos his arm for the two steps of his porch to the front door.

"Thank you, son. I haven't been to church since Alma passed. It was good to see everyone again."

"It was my pleasure." And it had been. It was fascinating to be the one interpreting for Amos. There had been a few hiccups along the way, but nothing terrible. And although initially people had assumed Malachi could hear, when he'd set them straight, they'd rolled with it. Maybe...maybe the people at Grace Fellowship just needed time. The folks at Arcadia Valley Community had been exposed to Amos, so seeing someone sign hadn't jarred them at all. And the group of seniors who had gathered for lunch at the Jukebox afterward had been a riot. "Let me know if you want to go again. I'm happy to take you."

Amos shook his head. "Maybe every now and then, but you belong with people your own age, not stuck with an old man. And I don't mind church on the television. I turn on the captions and don't have to worry about a thing. Plus I can pause if I have to use the facilities."

Malachi grinned. "Okay."

Amos rested his hand on Malachi's shoulder. "I don't know what happened with you and your young lady, but I saw her unloading a suitcase from her car yesterday. Figure that means she went on a little trip. But she's back now, and the only way you work through things is if you talk about them."

Malachi let his gaze wander across the street to Ursula's house. Her car was in the driveway. Was she home or had she walked somewhere? She liked to walk. What would he say, anyway? "I'll talk to her. But I need to figure out what to say, first."

"Start with 'I'm sorry' and go from there. Even if you don't think you're wrong." Amos' eyes sparkled with humor. "Take it from someone who was married more than sixty years; an apology is never a bad idea."

"I'll keep that in mind. Text me if you need anything, okay?"

Amos nodded. "Tell me how it goes when you get up the gumption to make your move."

Malachi scoffed. Gumption indeed. He waved as he trotted down the steps to his car. He had the gumption. But that wasn't going to be enough. What he needed was a plan.

He let his mind wander as he drove back to Corban's farmhouse. Maybe one of his brothers would have an idea. Or Ruth. But he'd rather save her for a last resort. She already had little hearts floating around her head all the time. And maybe he'd entertained that notion, briefly, about Ursula. But at this point they had to get back to being on speaking terms before anything else.

He turned into the driveway and sighed. Ruth and Corban were wrapped in each other's arms under the big tree out front where they often picnicked. They made a nice picture. Nicer because he knew there was genuine affection there, and friendship, not just romance. He shut off the engine and opened the car door. He'd just try to sneak past and leave them be. He got out, collected his Bible and phone, and shut the car door.

They jolted apart.

Malachi winced. "Sorry."

Ruth signed. "It's okay. I actually wanted to talk to you."

"Okay?" He wandered closer. They needed to get a picnic table, or something, for out here. It would make a nice spot to sit and read. "What's up?"

"January sixth." Ruth glanced up at Corban and he grinned as he nodded.

"What about it?" Malachi scratched his chin. Were they playing some kind of game where you randomly shouted out dates? If so, he was beaten. That date didn't ring any bells. Not that he was great at remembering dates, but he usually managed not to forget birthdays.

"Our wedding date. After Christmas and New Year's, though we did toy, briefly, with both of those dates. Ultimately, we decided it was better to have a day completely to ourselves. But we needed it to be in the winter, not only because it's calmer here on the farm, but the B&B is likely going to be considerably less busy, so closing for a couple of weeks won't be a problem." Ruth twined her fingers through Corban's. "And I'd like to thank you for bringing it to my attention that we needed to settle on something."

He winced, his gaze flicking to Corban. "Sorry, man."

"Don't be." Corban shook his head. "Needed to be done. I should've said something instead of stewing. I'm working on it."

Ruth leaned up and kissed his cheek. "We'll both work on it."

"That's only what, four months?" Malachi frowned. He didn't know much about wedding planning, obviously, but that seemed like a fast turnaround.

"We're keeping it small. It should be okay. But...could you help me work on Jonah about the cake?" Ruth turned puppy dog eyes on Malachi.

"Is he giving you the 'I'm not a pastry chef' line?" Malachi frowned. His brother was stubborn. But he could make a mean cake when he felt like it. Seemed like his sister's wedding was exactly the kind of time you should choose to feel like it. "I'll talk to him."

"You're the best." Ruth kissed Malachi's cheek. "Now go away. I wasn't finished kissing my fiancé."

Corban rolled his eyes and wrapped his arms around her waist.

Before Malachi could turn, Ruth touched his arm. "I had lunch with Ursula after church today. She was looking for you."

His heart skipped a beat. Maybe two. His sister had turned back to Corban. He wasn't going to get any more information out of her now. Maybe he didn't even want to. He'd have to pray about it...think on it. Like he had any choice about that.

By Wednesday, Malachi wasn't any closer to figuring out what to do. He'd read the email Ursula had sent agreeing to stay on as their web designer on Monday. He'd nearly gone over to see her right then, but he still wasn't sure what to say. So, instead, he'd sent along the short list of tweaks that he'd put together. And signed it Micah. His brothers had called him a chicken, but that was a small price to pay.

He breathed in the scent of baking and his mouth watered. The muffin of the week was cooling on the far counter. Malachi pointed and lifted an eyebrow.

Jonah sighed but waved him on.

Malachi grabbed a muffin and bit into it. French toast. Who knew you could make French toast muffins? He snuck a second muffin and wandered back into the office. He had to give Jonah credit for coming up with interesting ideas on the muffin front. But, pulling up the orders, he frowned. As good as these were, they weren't a runaway success. Maybe their copywriting needed a little help? Was there a better way to have described them in the newsletter that would've encouraged people to give them a try? He polished off the first and broke the second apart, reveling in the scent of the steam as it rose. It could use a touch of syrup.

Jonah waved as he entered the office and dropped into a chair. "Good?"

"Did you consider adding a touch of syrup?" Malachi offered the other half of the muffin to Jonah.

"Thought about it. Wasn't sure how it'd hold up when it was cooked. Guess I could give it a shot in the next batch." Jonah nibbled the muffin and held Malachi's gaze. "You hear Ruth finally set a date?"

"January. It's good. There's no need to wait when you're sure."

Jonah sighed. "She wants me to make her cake."

"And you should."

"Seriously?" Jonah shook his head. "I thought I might get a little understanding from you. You realize we're going to be dressed up like penguins and standing up front with her, right? How am I supposed to be in charge of a cake when I'm in the wedding party?"

Malachi shook his head. "Please. You manage more than that on a given day in this bakery. And you did more than this on a typical day when you were working the line. You'll be fine."

Jonah's shoulders fell. "I guess. I'm glad she's getting married. I like Corban. I just..."

"Need to make her cake."

"Yeah, all right." Jonah rubbed the back of his neck. "We might need to close for a day or two beforehand. You'll need to let everyone know ahead of time to pick up earlier in the week."

Malachi smiled. "That's easy. We'll need to figure out pickups for the people who use the farmers market soon, too, so they know what to do when the market closes for the season."

Jonah nodded. "I'm happy to leave that in your capable hands. You talk to Ursula yet?"

What was it with his siblings? "Not yet. I'm...not sure what to say."

"You're over thinking. Box up some muffins and go over there. Now. Seriously." Jonah stood. "And tell me how she likes them."

Malachi sighed. "You're sure?"

"When it comes to women, there's no way to be sure. But I know sitting in here moping isn't doing anyone any good."

"I'm not moping. I was coming up with a plan."

Jonah shook his head. "Sure you were. It involved a box of muffins and a conversation."

Malachi pursed his lips. Maybe his brother was onto something. And that conversation could start with "I'm sorry." Because Amos wasn't wrong about that. An apology was never a bad idea.

Malachi swallowed the bile that was trying to creep up his throat. It was because his stomach was churning. But he could do this. He had to. He caught sight of Amos out of the corner of his eye as he walked down the street. The old man gave him a thumbs-up. Did that mean Ursula was home? Or was it just general encouragement? Either way, it bolstered his spirits and quelled a little of the nausea swirling inside him.

He climbed the steps to Ursula's porch and waved to Triton. The cat was in his usual perch in the front window. He didn't yowl or hiss. Maybe that was a good sign, too. He pressed the doorbell and took a step back.

Triton shot Malachi an unimpressed look and hopped down, stalking out of view. Maybe it was better not to try and see signs in cat behavior.

Ursula peeked through the window to the side of the door. Her eyebrows shot up and she brushed at the T-shirt with a phone number from an old pop song emblazoned across its chest. She pulled open the door and offered a weak smile before signing, "Hello."

Malachi extended the box of muffins and waited for her to take them. When his hands were free he signed without speaking. She could keep up. And if she couldn't, well, she could ask a question. "I brought you these as an apology. I'm sorry I hurt you. I appreciate you continuing on with the website until we can find someone else."

"You don't have to find someone else. Unless you want to. But I hope you won't. I—I was hasty. I'm sorry, too." She glanced over her shoulder before opening the door wider. "Would you like to come in? Maybe we could talk?"

Malachi shook his head. "Thanks, but I can't. I have another delivery to make."

She was adorable when she was confused. Commenting on it probably wouldn't do him any favors though. He gestured to the bakery bag sitting at his feet.

"Oh. Okay." Ursula swallowed visibly. "Another time?"

He nodded. The right thing to do, probably, was to suggest a date that would work. But he'd gotten the inkling of a plan as he'd walked over, and, for now at least, maybe it was better to keep her guessing. "I should go. I really am sorry I hurt you."

Malachi bent to pick up the bag. He waved it in a jaunty salute, ignoring the fact that her lips were moving. He trotted down the steps and crossed the street.

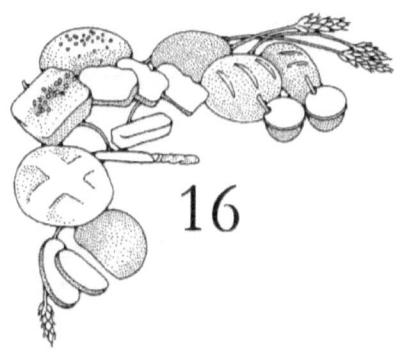

# 16

Ursula stood in the door and watched as Malachi crossed the street and climbed the stairs to Mr. Greenway's house. The old man grinned more brightly than she'd ever seen him as Malachi dragged a second lawn chair over and sat, offering the man the bakery bag. And then he started to sign. And Mr. Greenway signed back. Heart heavy, Ursula retreated into her house and closed the door. She wasn't going to eavesdrop. She'd never bothered to try and talk to the man, so of course she didn't realize he was deaf—maybe he was just hard of hearing? Although, would you learn to sign if you didn't need to? She had. For a friend. There was simply no way to know unless she took the time to meet her neighbors. Why hadn't she?

She swung into the kitchen for a glass of water. The answer was simple enough: she'd been happy in her isolated, online life. Malachi had shattered that. And as much as that hurt, it was a good thing. It was time. She popped open the box and considered the muffins inside. Three looked almost like bread pudding with a crumbly topping of some sort and three had...were those raisins?

Chocolate chips? She bet on chocolate and took one of those, flipping the lid down and tucking it in to keep Triton from poking his nose into all of them. Should she refrigerate them?

With the muffin and her drink, she went back to her office. The list of changes she'd gotten from the bakery was minor enough, but the database one was giving her a bit of a fit. Databases were someone's little joke on the computer world. Oh, sure, they served a purpose. But that didn't mean she had to enjoy working with them.

She took a bite of the muffin and sighed. So good. Like an oatmeal chocolate chip cookie but in muffin form. It was a sweet gesture. If only he'd stayed for a bit so they could talk. She had things she needed to say—a more complete apology to offer. Was he still across the street? Should she go over and ask...no...he probably had other deliveries beyond Mr. Greenway. Or work to do back at the bakery. And she had work to do, too. In spite of that, she found herself standing at the front window looking across the street. Mr. Greenway sat on his porch alone, munching on a muffin. Well, then. She'd get back to work, too. This was good. Better. Except she hadn't missed that Malachi didn't offer a suggestion for when to get together to talk.

The rest of the week passed in a blur of work and Orion's Quest with her dad. Ursula had checked every night to see if Malachi would sign in. But he hadn't. Would he really walk away from everything online, even after they'd—well, it wasn't all completely resolved, but they'd started toward that goal, hadn't they? Which left her pacing her living room on Sunday morning waiting for it to be time to leave for church.

She didn't need to be the first person who showed up. That...was just a little too desperate. If she caught him as he arrived, or just afterward, would he sit with her? She groaned. She was thinking about this entirely too much. Church was for Jesus. And if she was this focused on Malachi, she was going to miss out. *Jesus? Could you help me calm down, please? And...I know I've asked this a zillion times, but please fix things between Malachi and me. I don't know if more than friendship is what You want for us. I hope so. But I don't know. Even if it isn't...I'd really like to be friends with him.*

Ursula took a deep breath and grabbed her Bible and the notebook she used for sermon notes. Forget Malachi. She was going to go, get a seat, and focus on the service. And if she saw him...well, she'd cross that bridge when she got to it.

The morning showed the makings of another lovely day ahead. She slipped into her car and set her things on the passenger seat. She could walk...but having the car gave her the freedom to do whatever she wanted after church. Like maybe meet Malachi somewhere for lunch. Meet him instead of go with him. That kept it more casual. Friendly. No pressure. Her lips tingled as she remembered their kisses. *Oh, please, don't let those be out of the picture for good.*

Mr. Greenway wasn't out on his porch yet. Normally he was an early riser, out on the porch by the time Ursula shuffled into the kitchen for her first cup of coffee. Was he at church this morning? He didn't usually go. Or so it seemed. She hadn't always paid a ton of attention to what days were Sundays versus the rest of the week. Streaming the service from South Carolina meant she could do it live or wait and get to it on a completely different day if she needed to. Yet another thing she'd realized she needed to fix during her visit home. Her mom's point about needing community—one made up of real, live people—was valid. Which was, of course, why she was pulling into a parking spot at Grace Fellowship this morning instead of snuggling in bed with Triton and her laptop.

Triton didn't seem to care.

She took the bulletin from the usher standing by the door and scanned it as she scooted toward an empty seat in the middle of the sanctuary.

"Hey."

Ursula set her things aside and looked up. "Hi, Ruth."

"You want to come sit with us?" Ruth jerked her head toward the seats a few rows up where her brothers and fiancé were sitting. Jonah and Corban had turned and were looking their way. Micah and Malachi remained facing forward resolutely.

"Um." She drew her lower lip between her teeth. She did want to. But did *he* want her to? Or was it going to bother him? This is exactly why Ursula had wanted them to talk on Wednesday when Mal had come by. "Are you sure it'd be okay?"

Ruth smiled. "You're my friend. You're allowed to sit with me even if my brother—one or more of them—is a bonehead."

Ursula chuckled, but her heart sank. Was his apology simply that? A willingness to admit he'd hurt her but no interest in moving forward and seeing what kind of relationship they might have? She'd live with that, if she had to. She really didn't want to. She grabbed her things and stood. "Okay."

Ruth clapped her hands together and scooted out so Ursula had room to follow. "Yay. It's good to have one more female to balance out all the men."

"Happy to help." Ursula sat on the other side of Ruth at the end of the row. Jonah looked over and smiled. She waved. Corban grinned and took Ruth's hand. Micah and Malachi still didn't look her way, but they signed to one another. The angle was odd and she couldn't quite make it out, but she couldn't stop the thought that they were talking about her.

The service was good. Would Micah translate the entirety of it to Malachi since it was about forgiving someone who wronged you? Because like it or not, she'd made assumptions and had been just as wrong as him. Maybe more, since she'd lashed out in anger. She sighed. Her temper was the bane of her existence. No matter how hard she tried, it was there, lurking under the surface, waiting for an excuse to erupt. Dad said she got it from her mother. Maybe she did. But Mom's was under control, most of the time. Maybe that was something that came with age and experience?

"You there?" Ruth waved a hand in front of Ursula's face.

Heat flooded her cheeks. "Sorry. Thinking."

"Lunch? I have a casserole in the oven—the timer should've kicked in about thirty minutes ago to get it cooking. Then just some simple sides. But there's more than enough, even with these four." Ruth pointed at the guys.

Ursula followed Ruth's finger and her gaze locked with Malachi's. He gave the tiniest shake of his head. She swallowed the lump that formed in her throat and widened her eyes to keep the burning tears from filling her eyes. "I—" She cleared her throat and tried again. "I should get home. Triton—my cat—is still punishing me for having left him last week. Thanks though."

Shoulders back, head high, Ursula collected her things and strode out of the church, her pace quickening after she got through the doors into the foyer. By the time she hit the parking lot, it was the closest to running she'd come since high school gym class, and the tears she'd tried to control were spilling down her cheeks.

Triton curled against her legs as Ursula clicked the remote looking for something that wasn't a wedding fiasco show to watch. Honestly. Couldn't the programmers find something that wasn't a constant reminder that she was single and likely to stay that way for the rest of her life? Oh goody. Zombies. She paused. It still beat weddings. She ran a hand down Triton's back. He purred and butted her hand with his head. Ursula smiled. At least someone loved her.

Loved.

She wasn't in love with Malachi. But she could see the potential for it. Especially once she added in what she knew of him from their time playing online. Say what you would about online friendships, in their case, they'd discussed real things. Important things. She'd shown him parts of herself that she hadn't revealed to anyone else for a long time. Which was probably why she'd reacted so badly when she'd found out he'd known who she was all along. Okay, not all along. But for long enough without saying something.

She let out a breath. She'd forgiven him for that, though. She needed to stop dwelling on it. Except for the fact that she missed him. It was an ache in her heart that simply couldn't be soothed.

"Should I tell him, T? Or would that make it worse?"

Triton looked up at her and offered a short set of meows. Approval? It wasn't his chiding tone, though to be fair, he usually only used that when she gave him dry kibble when he'd clearly stated a preference for the wet.

Ursula leaned forward and grabbed her phone off the coffee table. She thumbed open a text message and typed his name in the "to" field. But what did she say? She couldn't very well just say she missed him. That was...obnoxious. It put all the blame on him and didn't accept any responsibility for the fact that this whole scuffle was, at least partially, her fault. Go for friendly? Breezy? Why not. She tapped out a text and studied it then hit send.

"There. It's done. I just told him it was good to see him at church. That's true and not scary, right, T?"

Triton gave a cat version of a shrug and twisted his head to get her fingers petting where he wanted them. Ursula smiled. Why couldn't men be as easy as cats?

Her phone chimed. He'd replied. That was a good sign, right? She tapped open his message.

"Good to see you, too. Did you like the muffins?"

She smiled and scooted down a bit so she could prop her feet on the coffee table. If they were going to text, she wanted to be comfortable.

"I did. Was that French toast? Different. But good." She waited after hitting send. Would he respond right away? She missed their talks...maybe he did, too?

"Needed syrup, I thought. Next week is banana nut. Jonah is going crazy about using bananas since they're not local but the supermarket had a lot that had ripened past what they could sell and they let us buy them cheap. Since our leftovers go to Corinna's Cupboard, everyone still wins and Ben doesn't have to deal with gross bananas."

Ursula smiled. She hadn't realized they donated their day-olds. That should go on the website. "Can I put day olds to Corinna's Cupboard on your About page? Think it's a major feel-good selling point for people."

Nearly five minutes elapsed between her text and Malachi's reply.

"Jonah says no thank you. Better to keep on the DL. Matt 6:3 and all."

She frowned and flipped to the Bible app, tapping in the verse. Huh. Good enough. "Well, I think it's cool. But that makes sense too. How are the muffins selling?"

"Only 2 weeks in. Hard to say. But I lean toward saying they're a good thing. They're starting to generate some walk-in business. Now thinking about coffee."

She laughed. If you give Arcadia Valley a muffin they are, most decidedly, going to want some coffee to go with it. "Talk to Grant Ward at the Beanery. He roasts here in town. Good stuff."

"Nice. Thanks."

Ursula waited. Finally, she changed the subject. "Couple of the guys on OQ asked about you coming back."

"Not sure if I will. Who?"

She gave him the names and added, "Hope you do."

When he didn't text back after five minutes, she set her phone down and dragged the blanket from the back of the couch over her. Triton gave a feline harumph and stalked into the kitchen. Ursula stretched out and gave her attention to the zombies. They might be enough

to keep her mind from wondering what Malachi was
thinking.

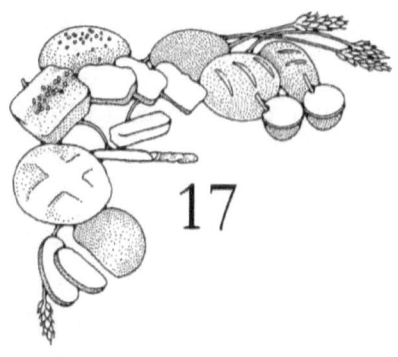

17

Malachi packed up the last box of bread and tucked it into the trunk of his car. Pick up day in Twin Falls had gone smoothly. He was starting to recognize the regulars, and word was getting out that he was there, so folks were stopping by for a one-off purchase. He had high hopes that they'd convert to a subscription. Jonah's baking had been good when they started the bakery in the spring and it was only getting better. The smaller items—muffins and cookies primarily—were good sellers down here. And at the register. Even Micah had to admit it.

Thursday night. Corban and Ruth would be having wedding planning discussions over their dinner tonight. Micah was probably reading some thick book published sometime around the invention of the printing press. And Jonah was more than likely ensconced at the computer flipping through recipes, looking for something to modify. As well as the muffins were selling, coming up with reasonable flavors seemed to stress Jonah out. Maybe once they got a decent number of good sellers figured out Jonah could just rotate through them. That might lift some of the pressure.

He got in the car and wound through the streets of the city—though calling it that still made him laugh. Twin Falls was nothing compared to Washington, D.C., or even the suburbs around it. Still, compared to Arcadia Valley it was bustling. He could go home and make a sandwich, close himself in his room and bounce around the Internet, or...he missed Ursula. Maybe he should do something about that. Their text conversation on Sunday had been pleasant, and the fact that she'd asked about OQ was encouraging. Not that he planned to play again anytime soon. There were questions he needed to answer first—because he still wasn't convinced he'd done anything wrong not mentioning his hearing.

He pulled into the parking lot of El Corazon. They had a decent crowd for Thursday evening from the looks of things. Hopefully it wouldn't take too long to get carry out. If Ursula had already eaten, well, he'd have leftovers for tomorrow night, too. Mexican was never a bad idea. He placed his order and sat in a chair by the door while he waited. Taking his phone out of his pocket, he texted his siblings to let them know his plan. Ruth had started a group text two or three years ago and it was still going strong, even now that they lived within five minutes of each other. Though it had transitioned to funny pictures half the time or snarky thoughts Micah had while sitting out front in the bakery and bored between customers. Or, like now, a chance for his brothers to send stupid comments like "Hubba hubba." Honestly, who said that anymore? He sent back an eye rolling emoji and tucked his phone back in his pocket.

Within fifteen minutes, Malachi had boxes of chicken and cheese enchiladas, along with beans and rice, and was back in the car. The rich scent of chicken and spicy sauce made his mouth water. He turned down the street and glanced at Amos' house as he drove past. The old man had gone inside already—probably time for his own dinner. It was good to know that he didn't sit out 'til all hours. Arcadia Valley was safe enough, but the man was older and could still catch a chill as the evenings cooled. He made a U-turn and pulled alongside the curb in front of Ursula's house. He grabbed the takeout and a box of muffins and took a deep breath.

Triton was missing from his usual perch in the window. Was it dinner time for cats, too? Malachi pushed the doorbell and fought the urge to shift from foot to foot. Ursula peeked through the sidelight window and grinned, pulling open the door. "Hi there."

Malachi lifted the bag emblazoned with El Corazon's logo and, as his hands were full, just spoke. "I was hoping you might be free for dinner."

Her eyes lit up and she pushed the door wider. "You just caught me. I was eyeing the peanut butter. I have to say, what you brought smells a lot better. Come on in."

Malachi followed her to the kitchen and smiled at Triton, who was hunched over his bowl chowing down on his kitty food. "I wondered why he wasn't in his usual spot in the window."

"Oh, no. He never misses a meal. Gets really cranky if I try to stretch him past five thirty." She pointed to the table. "Have a seat. I'll grab plates."

He set the muffins on the counter by the stove before pulling out a chair. He reached into the bag to get the two boxes of food. They didn't really need plates. But if she wanted to fuss, he wasn't going to stop her.

She touched his arm. "I have water or iced tea."

"Tea is good. Thanks." Malachi opened one container and breathed in the heady scent before tipping the contents onto a plate. He repeated the process with the other box, trying to keep everything from running together into a messy puddle.

"Ohhh. Enchiladas." Ursula leaned over her plate and sniffed before looking at him with a smile. "You remembered."

He nodded and reached for his tea. He'd tried to forget.

"I should probably warn you..." Ursula trailed off as he took a sip and made a face. "It's sweet tea. I went home after we fought. Mom reminded me how to make it the South Carolina way. I can get you some water."

"No. This is fine. I just wasn't prepared." He took another sip and set it down. For sweet tea it was delicious. And he didn't mind sweet tea. He just needed to know what he was getting. 'Cause when you were expecting unsweet, it was a bit of a shock. "There are a few places in D.C. that served it like this."

"Really? Seems like that'd be too far north."

He shrugged. It wasn't every restaurant, but it was often enough that he'd learned to specify when he ordered. He reached a hand across the table. "Can we say grace?"

She looked at his outstretched hand and her eyebrows lifted, but she laid her hand in his.

Malachi smiled and bowed his head, focusing all his attention on the words he wanted to say rather than how very *right* it was to hold her hand. He said "amen" and squeezed her fingers before retrieving his hand. The warmth of her touch, however, stayed with him.

"I think I finally conquered the database issue you were having." Ursula shook her head as she cut into the enchilada. "Shouldn't have taken me as long as it did. I've run into this before. This time, though, I made myself a note in the standard issues document I keep. Hopefully in the future I won't need to beat my head against the wall for several days."

"Thanks. It's a great site. You did a wonderful job." He scooped a bite of beans. It was still a little awkward. Was it better to just dive in? Probably. "I'm sorry I didn't stay the other day. And Sunday—the lunch thing—I had this plan but, I don't know, I think maybe this is better."

"I don't know. What was the plan?" She grinned and took another bite of her food.

Malachi frowned. Was she teasing him? She was. Had to be. He shook his head. "Don't remember. I really am sorry. I—the deaf thing—I'm not sure what happened there. I don't try to hide it. Except moving here, I do more talking without signing because when I sign people stare. And it's not like they sign. So. I wasn't trying to hide anything."

"No. I know that."

"The game thing though? That...I guess I was hiding. I'm not sure why. It was fun, I guess, to know both facets of you. Like a secret. I should've asked when I figured it out. Except at first, I wasn't sure. And if I was wrong, I didn't want you to think I was a big nerd—or worse, some kind of socially inept, immature loser who spent all his time playing games online because he was incapable of living in the real world." Malachi reached for his tea. He didn't want her to think that of him, but sometimes it felt true. Walking away from the game was harder than he'd anticipated. And that was troubling.

Her hand closed around his. "It's all right. I overreacted. I mean, I still wish you'd said something. But some of that is because I didn't want you to think those same things about me. And I was mortified thinking about the conversation we'd had about kissing. I wish I'd handled it differently. I'm sorry I didn't."

Malachi flipped his hand over and wound his fingers through hers. "Forgive me?"

"Absolutely. You'll forgive me?"

He nodded.

Ursula picked up her fork and took another bite.

Malachi sighed and tugged his hand free. "Sorry. I can't eat left handed."

Jonah was running wheat berries through the mill when Malachi got to the bakery on Friday. Usually he did that while they were closed. He said the sound carried out into the customer area. Malachi lifted a hand in greeting and bypassed the office to see Micah.

"Hey."

Micah set aside his book. "You're so lucky you can't hear."

Malachi grinned. "Why's he doing flour now?"

"Big special order just came in for an evening pickup. It won't be a problem to make the extra, but we didn't have enough flour for Jonah to be comfortable getting started."

Malachi reached for the scrap of paper that held the details. "This is all you wrote up?"

Micah nodded. "I figured you had a special form or something on the computer and could make a more official invoice before they came."

"Did you get a deposit?"

"Was I supposed to?"

"With an order this big? Yes." Malachi dropped the note on the counter in front of Micah. "Call him back and get fifty percent. 'Cause if Jonah makes that much extra and he's a no-show? It's bad news."

Malachi went back into the kitchen and waved to catch Jonah's eye before signing. "Don't start on that special order just yet. Micah's getting a deposit."

Jonah nodded and continued watching the wheat process into flour.

In the office, Malachi booted the computer and clicked open the email. He scrolled down through the spam—aha—he clicked open the message from the same name as what Micah had written down. And he said he was happy to pay a deposit, so that was good. Micah calling back shouldn't be too big a wrench in the works. If Malachi knew his brother, Micah would blame it all on him and spin some kind of woebegone tale of Malachi's overly-organized ways that would have the customer laughing while he read off credit card details. Everyone would end up happy.

Malachi transferred the information from the email into the accounting software and snapped a photo of it that he then texted to Micah. Hopefully he'd get it in time to tell the guy the right amount for the deposit. After a moment, his phone vibrated in his hand. Malachi looked down to see a photo of the cash register with the correct amount on the display. He shook his head. His brother was a moron.

He marked the deposit on the invoice and printed two copies. He left one on the kitchen counter by the list of shares that were due to be picked up today and gave Jonah a thumbs-up. Then he carried the other copy out front and handed it to Micah.

"Staple the receipt for the..." Malachi trailed off as Micah beat him to it.

"Not completely useless here in the front, you know." Micah grinned. "The guy was really nice, though he might think you're a pain to work for."

Malachi scoffed. "Figured. That's okay. Someone has to keep business in mind. Speaking of...I got a quote from the Beanery. For coffee? I think we should do it. He's roasting fair trade beans here in town. I bought some, figured I'd brew a pot in the back for us to taste in a minute. When I'm back in the office, I'll price out a few of the big dispensers, but we might need to have a counter and water hookup put in on the far wall to make it less of a hassle."

"That sounds potentially expensive."

The counter probably wouldn't cost much. Corban was pretty handy. Between the three of them they could make it look good enough. And if they couldn't, there were contractors in town. The water line was another story. "The alternative is making the coffee in the kitchen and lugging the full urns to the front every couple of hours."

"Price it out. It's not that hard to move urns around, and it'll give you and me something to do." Micah grinned and reached for his book. "If Jonah needs help, let me know. I'm game to do more in the kitchen and have you take a turn up front if that's what needs to happen."

Malachi nodded. He'd avoided taking shifts at the counter since Ursula had accused him of hiding his deafness. When he waited on customers, he had to speak. And read lips. Otherwise what was he supposed to do?

He'd gotten along fine like that in D.C. He could do it again here. He wasn't *hiding* anything...and she'd apologized. He needed to let it go.

It didn't change the fact that up front was his least favorite place to be. Scratch that. Helping bake would be his least favorite. So...up front it was if they needed all hands on deck.

Malachi sipped his coffee and watched the door. The special order was nearly ready, but the daily pickups had gotten behind schedule so Micah was in the back helping out. It had to be serious for Jonah to risk missing his three o'clock visitor. She ought to be along any second.

Sunlight flashed off a car window as a police cruiser turned into one of the parking spaces. She really was just like clockwork. And she looked good in uniform. She wasn't Ursula, by any stretch of the imagination, but she was definitely Jonah's type.

Gloria pulled open the door and stepped in. She took her customary sniff and smiled. "Hi there. Malachi, right?"

He nodded and stood. "Good memory. What can I get you today?"

Gloria scanned the offerings, her gaze drifting toward the door into the kitchen. Malachi fought a smile. Apparently the interest wasn't one-sided. "Are those rolls the cheesy ones?"

"They are—I think there's more than just asiago this time. Cheddar, too, if I recall." Malachi used tongs to grab one of the rolls and inspect it. "Yeah. That looks right."

"Mmm. That sounds perfect. I'll take one of those. What's the cookie today?"

"Snickerdoodles."

"Really?" Her eyes lit up. "I haven't had those in ages. I'll take one of those as well."

"Sounds good. How's your day been?" Malachi slipped the cookie and roll into a bag and rang her up. "Quiet, I hope."

She smiled. "It's always quiet. That's why I like working here. Everyone—thing—okay here?"

"We got a big special order this morning. Ten extra loaves and three dozen muffins. It set Jonah back a little, so Micah's gone back to help out."

Her face fell. "Oh. Well, a big order is good, right?"

Malachi took the bills she offered and made change. "It is. Word's getting out. That's never bad. Would you like some coffee? I made a pot from beans I bought at the Beanery. It's the best coffee I've ever tasted. We're considering serving it, so another set of tastebuds would be welcome."

"Yeah? Okay. Thanks." She took her bag to the table and sat.

"How do you take it?"

"Just black."

Malachi nodded and slipped into the kitchen. He tapped Jonah on the shoulder. "Take a mug of the coffee—black—out for Gloria and give yourself ten minutes. I can do this."

"You're sure?" Jonah frowned at the bowl of batter and the muffin pans.

How hard could it be? You scooped and plopped. He waved Jonah off. "Go."

Micah slid a tray of loaves into the oven. "I can do it. You probably have email to check or something."

"I do. Positive?"

"Shoo. I could be finished by now."

Malachi shook his head and went into the office. There wasn't any email that needed to be taken care of. Should he text Ursula? And say what? He frowned and opened a new text. Maybe Amos would be up for some Friday night company. The old man had promised him a game of checkers.

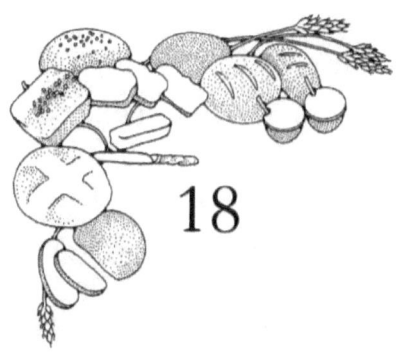

18

"Why am I here, again?" Ursula looked around the bridal shop in Twin Falls. So much white satin. And lace. And sparkling tiaras.

Ruth bounced on the balls of her feet. "Because I'm not bringing my brothers or my fiancé with me. You're the only female friend I have in Arcadia Valley. Besides, you said yes."

"Miss Baxter?" A slender, older woman in a sleek dusty rose suit approached from the back of the store. "I'm Barbara, your consultant. Who do you have with you?"

"This is my friend, Ursula." Ruth nudged Ursula's arm.

Ursula shook Barbara's hand. Friends? Were they? Was it that simple? With Ruth, it seemed to be. "Hi. I'm a little out of my depth."

Barbara laughed, a quiet, tinkling sound. "That's what I'm for. Come on back and let's talk a little about what Miss Baxter is looking for. All you need to do is be moral support."

"You can call me Ruth. Please."

"Can I get you some iced tea? Or maybe hot? Coffee? A cookie?" Barbara led them to a sitting area where a love seat was flanked by two Louis XVI chairs in matching pale pink satin.

"Um. Iced tea is good." Ursula debated the relative merits of chair versus love seat.

Ruth pulled Ursula down next to her on the settee. "That sounds good. And I never say no to a cookie." When Barbara smiled and strode off, Ruth clapped her hands. "This is so exciting."

"Okay. If you say so." It was all so fussy and female. She didn't have anything against either of those things, usually. But wedding stuff with Malachi's sister created a yearning in her heart that she wasn't sure what to do with.

"Maybe we'll be here for you before much longer." Ruth shot Ursula a knowing grin. "Heard you had some Mexican food. How was it?"

"Enchiladas are never a bad thing."

Ruth laughed. "You're terrible. I didn't mean the food. Has my brother stopped being an idiot?"

"He never started." Ursula held up a hand to stop Ruth from speaking. "Seriously. It was...basically all me. But I think we have it figured out and can be friends now."

"Friends?" Ruth's expression settled into a mask of disappointment.

"Friends." It would be enough, somehow. He'd held her hand, but that was just to pray. And if he'd felt any of the same things she did, he hadn't shown it. So...friends.

Ruth watched her for a moment then sighed. "I guess you have to start somewhere."

Barbara glided back in with a tray that she set on the small pouf in the center of the seating and took a chair. "Here we are. Now, Ruth, tell me what you're picturing for your special day."

Ursula listened with half an ear as Ruth described her plan for a simple, homey wedding at Grace Fellowship in January. It sounded...lovely. Nothing ornate or over the top, just two people pledging their love before God and man. It wasn't what she'd expected from someone who came from Washington D.C. But then, the wedding wasn't going to take place there, so maybe Ruth was simply good at adapting to her environment. Or maybe she'd finally found the environment that suited her.

"January. Well. We do have our work cut out for us." Barbara tapped her lips with her index finger. "There should still be time for all the fittings but I'm glad you came in when you did. Now, tell me about your dream dress."

Ruth tensed up. "I...need a little help there, to be honest. All I know for sure is that I want white and it has to have sleeves."

"You're not thinking of an outdoor wedding?" Barbara's expression bordered on horrified.

Ursula snickered. "I think it's more of a modesty thing. You'd be okay with lace or short sleeves, right? You just want to be covered?"

Ruth nodded.

"Ah. Hmm. I have a couple of ideas. Ruth, come with me. I'll pull a few dresses while you undress. Ursula, we'll be out to show you something in just a few minutes." Barbara stood and waited while Ruth nervously set her purse next to Ursula on the love seat. Ruth was pale.

Ursula fumbled for Ruth's hand and gave it a squeeze. "You'll be fine. I can't wait to see what she gets."

Ruth took a deep breath. "Okay."

Ursula picked up a glass of the tea and sipped. She made a face and spit most of the liquid back. There was a small bowl of sugar packets on the tray. She grabbed three and dumped them in, stirring forcefully before taking another sip. Better. But it was a stern reminder that she wasn't in South Carolina anymore. The cookies were tiny little store bought things. She should recommend the bakery. With Malachi doing deliveries down here once a week, the bridal shop could probably get a couple dozen, and they'd stay fresh enough to be better than these.

Unable to help herself, she stood and walked over to one of the dress racks. She flipped through the hangers and paused on a white satin gown with an empire waist. The bodice was quilted—almost medieval looking with the gold thread woven through the design—and the skirt fell loose and unadorned to the floor. There was a small train trailing from the back. It was...exactly what she'd choose if she were getting married anytime in the next century.

She flipped the price tag over. Not as dreadful as she'd imagined. Not cheap, but then, what wedding dress was? Still, it was nice to know that something affordable was still possible today. The TV shows made it look like you had to take out the equivalent of a car loan in order to be properly dressed for your wedding.

"Here we are. This is the first dress I pulled." Barbara clipped back into the room on heels that must leave her feet screaming by the end of the day. Ruth followed behind her, lost in the enormous full skirt of the dress.

Ursula shook her head. "No. That's...dreadful."

"Oh thank goodness." Ruth let out a breath. "I was afraid it was just me."

"No. That's the perfect dress for someone who's eight inches taller than you and into drama. But it does have sleeves. So, bonus points."

Barbara offered a tight smile. "All right. Let's go try the next one."

Ursula pressed her lips together. Was she not supposed to be honest? That's what Ruth had said she needed in the car on the way down. Maybe Barbara just needed to loosen up a little. Ruth couldn't possibly be the only person who hadn't swooned at the first dress she tried on. She rubbed her hand down the dress she'd been looking at and tucked it back into the rack. There was no wedding in her future, so why was she even looking? She made her way back to the love seat.

This time, Ruth preceded Barbara into the room, her face alight. The dress had a sweetheart neckline, long lace sleeves, and an A-line skirt that fell in soft folds around her. There was a sparkling belt at the waist that added a little bit of drama and took the dress from prom to wedding. "Oh. Wow."

Barbara beamed and helped Ruth step up onto the round platform in front of a three-panel mirror. She fluffed the skirt and train and stepped back. "What do you think?"

Ruth ran her hand down the skirt and looked over her shoulder at Ursula. "I love it."

Ursula nodded. "You'd be insane not to."

"Should I try on more? Barbara pulled two others...I don't know the right answer."

"And I do? I've never been engaged." She'd never dated someone for more than three months. But that could be left unsaid. The point was the same. Ursula looked at Barbara. "What do you recommend?"

"Why don't I bring the other two dresses out for you to see? Maybe if you see them next to this one, you'll have an idea if she should try them on or not."

Ruth nodded. "That...sounds like a good idea."

Ursula stepped closer, lightly touching the material of the train. "This is really lovely. It's in your price range?"

"It is. Just. The first one was over by half, so I was actually quite pleased that it was terrible. I weeded through the others she pulled—there were eleven—and told her I wasn't looking at anything over a thousand dollars. I know in wedding-dress-land that's nothing, but I can't justify spending more than that on something I'm going to wear once." Ruth leaned back, her gaze shifting down the hall to where the dressing rooms were, her voice dropping to a whisper. "She wasn't happy, but she went along with it."

Ursula nodded.

Barbara returned holding two dresses. She hooked one on the edge of a rack and climbed up to stand by Ruth with the other. The contrast was stunning. Where the dress Ruth had on was understated and elegant, the one on the hanger was over-the-top with sparkles and a fluffy princess skirt.

"Oh. I...no. I think you'd have the same problem with that one as the first. That skirt would eat you alive."

Ruth laughed. "That's...quite the mental image. But I tend to agree. I don't feel any desire to try that one on."

"All right." Barbara stepped back down and switched the dresses before returning to stand by Ruth. "What about this one?"

Ursula pursed her lips and moved so she could see it better. The dress was simpler—a column rather than an a-line. "It's a completely different look. I think you could pull it off though, if you wanted to."

"I looked at a lot like that online. Maybe...maybe I should try it." Ruth reached out and took the dress from Barbara, holding it in front of her. "Should I?"

"It doesn't hurt, and it's better to be sure."

Barbara smiled and reached for the second dress. "That's true. It's always better to be sure."

"Okay. You don't mind?"

Ursula shook her head. This was already going faster than she'd anticipated. Frankly, she'd expected the Twin Falls shop to be a bust and a road trip to Boise to be in the works for some weekend soon. If they could find a dress in one afternoon of shopping? That seemed miraculous.

When they disappeared back down the hall, Ursula returned to the rack and slid the hangers aside to reveal the empire waist gown once again. Checking to see that they were gone, she lifted the hanger off the pole and carefully stepped onto the platform, holding the dress in front of her. It was perfect. If only she had a groom. She pictured Malachi standing next to her in a charcoal tuxedo with a vest and tie rather than cummerbund. Tails? Definitely. He could pull them off. Her heart gave a lazy flip. What was she doing?

She jumped off the platform and fumbled to hook the hanger back on the dress rack.

"What did you find?"

Ursula turned at Ruth's question, heat warming her cheeks, and hummed in her throat. "That's...different. In a good way."

It was much more sophisticated. Definitely not the girl-next-door vibe the other dress gave off.

"It really is. But it's not who I am anymore. This would've been the perfect dress if I'd married Lars back in D.C. But for Corban?" Ruth shook her head. "This doesn't fit us at all. And I'm grateful for that. It really is lovely though."

Barbara smiled. "I concur. And you look stunning in both, but I tend to agree the first one is a better fit. You glowed."

"Pull that dress back out, Ursula. I want to see it."

"Don't be silly. I was just poking around while I waited."

Barbara made an impatient noise and crossed to the rack, her hand unerringly closing over the dress she'd been looking at. "This is lovely. And it would definitely suit you."

"Not engaged. Not even dating anyone." Ursula held her hands in front of her, fending off...well, everything. She wasn't trying on a wedding dress when she didn't have a boyfriend.

"Oh come on. It'll be fun. It's all right, isn't it Barbara? It wouldn't take long."

Ursula gave her friend a long look. She hadn't realized the woman was a champion wheedler. "I really don't—"

"Come on. Ruth's right, it'll be fun. And you might be the first person to try this one on that I think it actually suits. It's eye catching, and affordable, so a lot of mothers pull it. But it never really fits." Barbara hoisted the dress to keep it from dragging on the floor.

"Yay!" Ruth stepped down from the platform, wobbling a little as the column restricted her movement.

"I'll put my regular clothes back on and meet you back out here."

Ursula sighed and followed Barbara. She should've stayed in her seat. Or at least not taken the dress down off the rack. Now...there was little choice. Barbara held open a dressing room door and followed her inside.

"Have you tried on a wedding dress before?"

Ursula shook her head.

"Go ahead and take your clothes off. It's generally better to step in, although this one can go over the head without too much fuss if you prefer." Barbara worked to take the dress off the hanger.

Ursula swallowed. The woman was staying in here with her? It was worse than high school gym class. At least then the other girls had also been busy changing. Barbara just stood, looking at her impassively. She closed her eyes and took a deep breath before tugging off her clothes and crossing her arms over her middle.

"Here, step in." Barbara held out a hand.

Ursula did as instructed and slid her arms into the sleeves as Barbara pulled the dress up, adjusting and fussing as she did so. The back was fastened with buttons. The woman must have the world's most nimble fingers, because she had it closed in record time.

"There now. Have a look."

Ursula turned and looked at herself in the mirrors. The dress fit like it had been made for her. And it was even better than she'd imagined it. Tears welled in her eyes. She blinked them back. "Wow."

"Mmm. It definitely suits you. You're sure you don't have someone on the horizon?"

Ursula managed a sardonic laugh. "Pretty sure."

"Too bad. Let's at least go show your friend."

"No. I don't think—"

"Don't be ridiculous. She wants to see." Barbara opened the dressing room door and arched a brow.

Fine. Okay. It was like playing dress up. That's all it was. Ursula strode down the hall to the front and paused. "See?"

Ruth turned, her jaw dropping. "Oh. Oh oh oh. Up on the platform. I need to see the whole thing."

"Come on, Ruth. This is dumb."

"Nope. Up."

Better to just get it over with. She stomped to the platform and stepped up. She wasn't going to imagine Malachi beside her this time though. Maybe, oh, that Australian actor who played in all the action movies. Ursula tried to conjure the image, but it kept morphing into Malachi and the charcoal tux. She sighed. "Okay, there you go. Can I change now?"

Ruth frowned, but she nodded. "You really do look lovely."

"Thanks." Ursula headed back down the hall with Barbara on her heels. The woman undid the buttons in the back and pointed at the hanger before disappearing. At least she got some privacy to change out of the dress. She gave the fabric a final, loving stroke after she hung it up and hurried back to the front of the store.

Barbara stood at the register. Ruth's dress hung in a bag by the counter. "Have you given thought to a veil or a headpiece?"

"I have my mother's veil."

Barbara smiled. "Lovely. If you need help with shoes, I hope you'll come back."

Ruth nodded and signed the credit card slip before putting the card back in her purse. "Thank you for all your help."

"If you decide you do want the hem raised a little, please call and we'll get you an appointment with the seamstress. I think you'll be fine as long as your shoes have a little heel, but it's what you'll be comfortable with that matters."

Ursula grabbed the dress off the hook and headed toward the car with a wave to Barbara.

"Hey." Ruth hurried up from behind. "You okay?"

"Yeah. I'm good." Other than that impossible fantasy of Malachi. Talk about rushing things and setting herself up for heartbreak.

"Want to grab an early dinner before we head back?"

Ursula shook her head. "I'm getting a headache...would you mind if I took a rain check?"

"Not at all. Let's get you home."

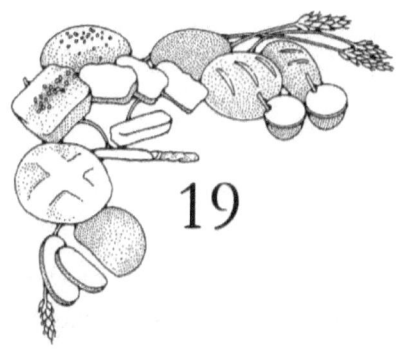

19

Malachi looked up from his phone when the light over the door flashed and caught his eye. What was Ruth doing stopping by this close to closing? "Hey. Weren't you going out this afternoon?"

Ruth grinned. "Already done."

"Really? I thought dress shopping was supposed to take longer than that." Malachi tucked his phone in his pocket and leaned forward on the counter.

"Maybe. But I bought the second dress I tried on. It's perfect. Bonus, it doesn't need any alterations."

"Cool." Since his sister had to know he couldn't possibly care less about her wedding dress—not that he wasn't happy she found one, but it didn't go much beyond that—there had to be some alternate reason for her to be here. How long would it take for her to get around to it? "Jonah and Micah already left. They were both looking beat."

"That explains why you're out front. I know you hate it."

He shrugged. "It's not that bad. I've decided I just need to sign when I speak so people understand why I miss something if they're not looking at me. I'm done being self-conscious about it, though. I am who I am, you know?"

"I'm so glad to hear you say that." She pulled her lip between her teeth. "Did the fight with Ursula have anything to do with this new realization?"

"A little. But we're good now. I told you that." Maybe they weren't back to where they had been. But who knew if that was even still possible? He'd like it to get there, but did she? It was hard to tell. Still, the ache that losing his daily conversations with her online caused had lessened and was now something he could, mostly, ignore.

"Define good. 'Cause I get the impression from Ursula that maybe that word doesn't mean what you think it does when it comes to relationships."

The light above the door flashed as one of their regular Monday pickups came in. Malachi collected the bag under the counter that held their standing order. "Hold that thought. Hi there, adding anything on?"

"Yeah, toss in a half-dozen of the muffins and two cookies, would you?" The woman smiled at her daughter who was spinning in circles. "Someone earned a treat. And mommy wants one too. Is there a way to just upgrade my weekly purchase to include the muffins?"

Malachi grinned. "Absolutely. I'll take care of that for you. Half-dozen each week?"

She nodded. "Please. We've loved every kind you've offered so far, so there's no reason to imagine we won't keep on doing that. Honestly, this week's apple-cinnamon are exactly the whisper of fall I've been craving."

"I'll let my brother know. That'll make him happy." Malachi boxed up the muffins and slid cookies into a bag before tucking them into the reusable bag they used for regulars. The woman set last week's bag on the counter and dug in her purse for her credit card. He tapped the reader. "Go ahead and sign. Do you need a receipt? We can email or text it if that's easier."

"A text would be great—I think I'm in the system already so it should have my details."

Malachi confirmed that and nodded before tapping the text receipt button. "There you go. Have a great day."

The mother and daughter left, the little girl still twirling.

Ruth walked over with a mug of coffee.

Malachi arched an eyebrow. "That'll be seventy-five cents."

"Add it to my tab." Ruth made a face before taking a sip. "So. Ursula?"

"We're friends, okay? I think that's how she wants it."

Ruth shook her head. "Bzzt. Try again."

He frowned. "We aren't friends?"

"Don't be dense, Mal. She doesn't want to just be friends. I'm not sure where you were on the relationship spectrum before whatever happened, but it's pretty clear to me that she'd like to be back to that point. At a minimum." She paused and took a sip from the mug. "She tried on a wedding dress this afternoon, too."

His heart raced. A wedding dress? He wasn't at the wedding dress stage yet. He took a breath. Then another. Why couldn't he get any air?

"Whoa there. I'm not saying she's going to ask you to marry her tomorrow. I'm just saying that she's got love—and forever—on her mind. I thought you did, too." Ruth's forehead creased. "Are you okay? You should sit down."

Malachi found the stool by the register and lowered himself onto it, still trying to catch his breath. The edges of his vision were fuzzy.

"Slow down. You're going to hyperventilate. What's going on?" Ruth came around the counter and rubbed his back.

He shook his head and took in a deep breath, holding it this time, before letting it out. Better. That was better. His heartbeat began to slow.

"Do you want some water?" Ruth stepped back and studied his face.

"I'm okay."

"You want to tell me what that was?"

Not really. Especially since he wasn't positive himself. He wanted more from Ursula than friendship. Their kisses haunted his dreams. But marriage was a few big steps down the road, and he hadn't even been sure they were still on it. It was the logical progression...but did you think about marriage before you knew you were in love? "It's nothing."

"Nothing. Got it. 'Cause you have—what was that, a panic attack?—all the time. I shouldn't have said anything. But I *like* Ursula. And she's good for you, whether or not you'll admit it."

He liked Ursula, too. Cared for her. He skirted around the l-word when it popped into his mind. Skipping steps had proved disastrous once already. But maybe it was time to nudge things up a bit from friends to something closer to what they'd had before. Or at least to try. "Okay."

Ruth rolled her eyes. "Box up a dozen muffins, would you? They'll be a nice addition to the breakfast buffet tomorrow morning."

"I'm sorry." He moved to the display case and loaded up a box.

"No. It's fine. I know guys don't spill their innermost secrets all the time. But you've always been a little more open with me than your brothers. I don't like feeling shut out."

He set down the muffins and took her hands in his. "I'm not shutting you out. I'm just...trying to figure out what's going on."

"I know. I'm sorry if I was pushy."

"You're always pushy. That's what older sisters do."

She grinned and offered him her credit card. "Don't you forget it."

Malachi locked the back door of the bakery and carried two small muffin boxes out to the car. It was hard to believe it was going to be September on Friday. The weather agreed. Temperatures had been steadily cooling from the nineties earlier in the month and had hovered in the high seventies today. Or so the weather app on his phone said. He hadn't actually gotten out of the store until just now. It was a lovely evening, though some clouds were moving in. Would it rain?

He got in his car and turned toward Amos' house. The man loved his muffins. And Malachi could use his advice. As much as he appreciated Ruth's attempt to talk with him, she was still his sister. And she was in the throes of her own happy ending. It was natural—from both standpoints—that she'd see the easy slip into love for Ursula and him. Maybe she was right—he hoped so—but he still wanted to see what Amos had to say.

Malachi parked along the curb in front of Amos's house and looked across the street. The light in Ursula's front room flickered—she must be watching TV. He left the box of muffins he'd brought for her on the front seat of his car. Maybe he'd swing by after he talked to Amos. Depending.

He took the stairs to the porch by twos and frowned. Why wasn't he still outside? Had he gotten chilly? Had his doorbell been adapted to flash a light somewhere he'd see it? Surely it had. Malachi pressed the bell. Seconds ticked by. Maybe he'd send a quick text to let Amos know he was here. He pulled out his phone and did that then waited.

When five minutes had gone by without a reply to his text or Amos at the door, a tiny tendril of worry wormed through him. He reached out and set his hand on the knob and stopped. What if it was unlocked, would he go in? And if there was nothing wrong? No. If there was nothing wrong, Amos would have texted back. He'd been quick to reply every time in the past. Malachi twisted the knob and pushed open the door. The fact that it was open did nothing for his hammering heart.

The house was dark. All the blinds were still closed. Malachi thought back to the times he'd visited on the porch with Amos and couldn't remember if that was usual. It didn't seem like it. Not for a man who could rhapsodize about the sunshine like Amos could.

There was no one in the kitchen. Or the living room. Malachi swallowed, but it did nothing for the desert in his mouth. He turned on the hallway light and looked down toward the bedrooms. Everything was neat, it didn't look like Amos had fallen or anything like that. He strode down the hall, peeking in the first door and continuing on when that room, too, was empty.

The door to the second bedroom was open. The lamp on the nightstand was on and Amos was tucked neatly in bed, his eyes closed. He looked small and frail. The importance of Amos' friendship slammed into him and tears blurred Malachi's eyes as he crossed the room. With a shaking hand, he reached out and gently shook his friend's shoulder. Amos' eyes fluttered open but they didn't latch on to Malachi's. Something was clearly wrong.

No. He couldn't die. Malachi sank to his knees and dropped his head to the side of the bed. Tears slipped down his cheeks. What was he supposed to do? He swallowed the lump in his throat and knuckled away his tears. For now...he needed help. He stood and, after one last look at his friend, hurried from the room.

He jogged across the street and rapped on Ursula's door.

She opened it a crack. "It's not a good time. I have a headache and—"

"Please. I need help." Malachi signed without speaking, his voice frozen in his throat. "It's Amos."

Confusion registered on Ursula's face, mixed with a trace of irritation. "Who's Amos?"

"Your neighbor?" Malachi pointed.

"Mr. Greenway?"

Malachi nodded. "He's really sick. Can you call an ambulance?"

Ursula didn't move for the space of several heartbeats then pushed the door open wider. "Come in. I'll grab my phone."

While Ursula punched in 9-1-1, Malachi signed a short version of what happened. She nodded and relayed a summary to the operator.

Malachi sank onto the couch and buried his face in his hands.

The cushion next to him gave way as Ursula sat. She laid her hand on his leg and rubbed.

When he looked up, she nodded out the window. "They asked us to meet them at the door. Are you—can you?"

He nodded and started to stand. Malachi looked over at Ursula and warmth pushed through the cold inside him. It was as if everything had been blurry and now, suddenly, had snapped into focus. "I love you."

The corners of her mouth twitched up, her eyes lighting. She touched her lips to his, just the barest brush, but it was enough. "Here they are. Come on."

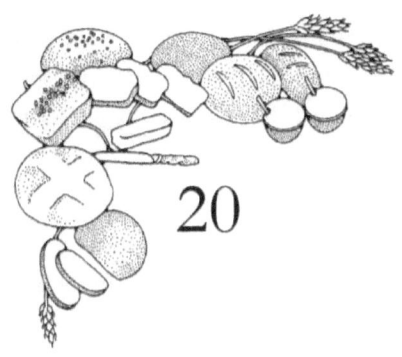

# 20

Ursula held Malachi's hand as he spoke to the policewoman on the sidewalk, explaining once again what had transpired, but her thoughts were jumbled. He loved her. She squeezed his hand. Was this love? It wasn't like in the movies. But then, what in life was?

The EMTs carried the stretcher down from the porch then rolled it to the ambulance. Malachi stiffened, his breath catching.

"Do you know who we should contact?" The officer, who'd introduced herself as Gloria, slipped a pen out of her shirt pocket.

"Not really. His wife already passed. But he said he texted his kids and grandkids...so I guess try his phone. I'm glad it's you who responded. I needed a friendly face."

Gloria put the pen back in her pocket and smiled. "We'll figure it out. It's good you went in. Cases like this, sometimes people go for awhile without anyone noticing. Since you found him, we can get him help and hopefully he'll be on his way to recovery soon."

"I don't think that would've happened to Amos. He has friends at his church who stop by. And his kids, like I said. And me." Malachi's eyes filled again and he turned his head away.

"Which church?"

Ursula bit her lip. Malachi wasn't watching, so he wouldn't have seen the woman ask her question. "I think he goes to Arcadia Valley Community. But I'm not positive."

"You're the neighbor?"

Ursula nodded.

"When was the last time you remember seeing him?"

"I'm pretty sure I saw him out on the porch this morning. He likes to sit out and watch the neighborhood. He wasn't there when I went out this afternoon though, around two?"

"Thanks." The policewoman touched Malachi's arm. "Hang in there, Malachi."

He nodded. "Thanks, Gloria."

She nodded and returned to her cruiser.

Malachi's shoulders hunched.

Ursula slipped her arm around his waist and waited until he met her gaze. "Come on. Let me fix you some supper."

"I'm not hungry."

"Just some soup. It'll warm you up. If you need more after that, I make a mean grilled cheese. I have this bread from a local bakery, maybe you've heard of them, A Slice of Heaven?"

The corners of Malachi's lips tipped up.

Her heart lifted. That was better. "It makes amazing sandwiches."

"I was going to surprise you after I talked to Amos."

She chuckled. "You still surprised me."

"I bet. You said it wasn't a good time. I can go. I know how to make soup."

"Please don't. I'd like you to stay. I've been thinking about you all day." That was a bit of an understatement when she considered how her thoughts had veered at the wedding dress shop. But the main idea was the same.

"Okay."

She pushed him toward the couch. "You sit. I'll make the food."

He nodded.

Chewing her lip, Ursula went to the kitchen. She dropped a scoop of kibble into Triton's bowl and reached for her phone. She'd text Ruth and let her know what happened. If he was her brother, she'd want to know. She made it clear that Malachi was okay. Then she went to the freezer and pulled out a glass jar. She'd made a big batch of chicken noodle soup in the spring and had stored most of it for the winter. This seemed like the perfect time to break some out. She took off the lid and put it in the microwave for just long enough to loosen the contents enough that she could scoop it out into a pan. Soup always reheated better on the stove.

Maybe after they ate, they could go down to the hospital and check on Mr. Greenway. That might help Malachi feel better. How late were visiting hours? She opened a browser on her phone and looked up the information. Hmm. They might not make it. But they could at least call and find out if Malachi could visit tomorrow.

The soup began to bubble. Ursula stirred it and dipped her finger in. Not quite hot all the way through, but getting there. She peeked into the living room. Malachi was on the couch, his head back, eyes closed. She'd never seen him look so exhausted. But he was still handsome. She smiled and, after turning the heat down, tiptoed into the living room. Half way across the floor she stopped and laughed. She didn't have to sneak. He wasn't going to hear her. She finished crossing to him and gently lowered herself into his lap.

Ursula laid her head on his shoulder. His arms came around her, holding her in place. Even as she relaxed into his embrace, every nerve ending was on fire. It was wonderful. And right.

He loved her.

She raised her head and met his gaze but the words lodged in her throat. Could she trust him enough to say them? Could she trust herself?

He smiled then, for a moment, before bringing his lips to hers.

Ursula waved to Malachi as he drove off. The sun had set and the evening air had cooled to the point that she rubbed her arms before closing the door. Her cell phone rang. She snagged it and accepted the call. "Hi, Mom."

"Hi, baby. How was your shopping trip with your new friend?"

Ursula chuckled. Leave it to her mother to latch onto not only the fact that she'd voluntarily gone shopping but that she'd managed to make a female friend as well. "It was good. Ruth found a dress, so I guess you could say it was a success."

"That was fast. Oh, honey, you didn't talk her into settling for something just because you hate shopping, did you? It's her wedding. She needs to feel like a princess. Maybe you should've made her wait until her own mother could go. Or a sister?"

"Nice to see you have confidence in me. As it happens, I did not make her settle. I even suggested she go ahead and try on another dress after she was ready to stop. She ended up going with her original pick, but at least this way, she knows for sure it's the right one. And she has brothers. No sisters that I know of." Ursula dropped onto the couch. She turned her face into the cushion and breathed in. There was a tiny lingering hint of Malachi's scent. She hadn't wanted him to go. But it was good he did. "Then Malachi came over for dinner."

"Oh?" Her mother had always been able to ask a number of questions with just one word.

Ursula filled her mom in on the events of the evening. "I called the hospital after we ate. He's been admitted and Malachi should be able to visit him tomorrow. They didn't say anything about what happened, but that's to be expected. Still, it's good Malachi decided to stop by and take him muffins."

"You said his name's Amos? I'll get him added to the prayer chain. It was nice of you to make him some dinner. It must've been a shock."

"I had a little shock myself."

"Of course you did. I'm sorry. He's your neighbor, after all."

"Not that, although yes." Ursula took a deep breath. Telling her mother was a big step. But why would she wait? It was the first time she'd ever felt this way. The first time anyone had felt this way about her. "Malachi told me he loves me."

"Oh, honey." Her mother sniffled. "I'm so glad. When you came home...I was worried about you. More worried after you left. But this young man...you love him?"

"I...how do you know? How did you know you loved Dad?"

"Hmm. I reached a point when I couldn't imagine my life without him. When even my worst day with him was better than the best day if he was missing. Beyond that? I chose it. I chose to love him. I still do, every day. Sometimes I think the world gives us this message that love is some mysterious vapor that you breathe in and catch like a virus, when what it really is, when you boil it all down, is a decision. Everything you've told me about Malachi says that he's a kind, smart, handsome man who loves Jesus. He's committed to his family and he's a hard worker. I couldn't ask for any better qualifications in a man for my daughter to love. Which brings us back to my original question. Do you love him?"

Did she? Was it really as simple as choosing? They had chemistry. And friendship. And the days when she saw or talked to him were so much better than the days without. "Maybe I do."

"Then maybe I'm happy for you."

Ursula chuckled.

"Bring him with you when you come for Thanksgiving."

Ursula laughed. She didn't even know if she was going home in November yet. Her unplanned trip had made a big dent in her travel fund. Sure, business was good, but that just meant she had enough to live on, not that she had enough to jet around the country all the time. "We'll see what I can do. I love you, Mom."

"Love you too. Keep me posted, okay?"

"Of course."

Ursula ended the call and hugged herself. In love with Malachi. He was her best friend—well, his online persona was. And now that she'd gotten to know him in person, even with their fight, that still held. She was more comfortable talking to Malachi than she'd ever been with anyone else. A choice. All things considered, it would be an easy one to make. Triton jumped up next to her and butted her arm with his head. She chuckled and rubbed him from his head to the tip of his tail. "I know, I know. Time for your treat, greedy boy."

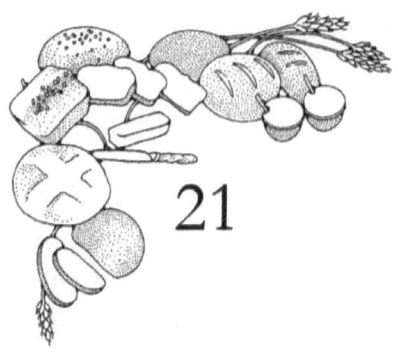

21

Malachi wrinkled his nose against the antiseptic smell of the hospital and glanced down at the paper holding Amos' room number. He carried a small green potted plant in his left arm along with a paper sack. Mrs. Akers, at Blossoms by the Akers, had assured him it was a good gift for someone in the hospital. It wasn't girly. That had been his primary concern. No man wanted flowers. A plant though, that could be manly. Or was Amos too old to care about manly? Maybe he liked flowers. It was too late now. He was getting a plant.

Malachi swallowed. There it was. He poked his head in the door. Amos sat watching the television with the captions on. He smiled when he saw Malachi and waved him in.

"I brought you a plant." Malachi set the pot on the table by Amos' bed and looked at his friend. "How are you?"

"That's a beautiful hosta. Thanks. I'm okay. Had a stroke, they're telling me. Also saying I owe you my life. So thank you. I'm grateful you stopped by."

Malachi nodded, noticing now the droop in the left side of the older man's face and the difficulty he had signing with both hands. "I don't want to tire you out, but I wanted to see you. Make sure you're okay."

"Don't go. It's horrible here. My daughter is on the way out, but she won't be here until tomorrow morning. And the sign language interpreter at the hospital is only around when the doctor makes his rounds, though they said they'd bring her whenever I wanted her. I don't want to be a bother. So the rest of the time, it's just me and the TV. I want to go home."

Malachi pulled a chair closer to the bed and sat. "I'm sorry. I can stay. I should have come in the ambulance with you last night."

"Don't be silly. I'm not even sure they would have let you. You're not kin. But if you can stay for a while now, I won't say no." Amos offered a weak, one-sided smile that left him looking like the old man he was.

"Of course. Just let me tell my brothers not to expect me back." Malachi pulled out his phone and texted Micah. They'd understand. Jonah had already suggested he take the rest of the day off. "There. One good thing did come of this."

"Yeah? What's that? I could use a silver lining."

"I told Ursula I love her. Seeing you that way...it all sort of came together. I want what you and Alma had. And I want it with Ursula."

Amos nodded. "Let an old man give you one more piece of advice?"

"Of course."

"Don't waste a lot of time waiting for it to be perfect. Pray about it, yes. But when you know for sure, ask her to marry you. And then get married and start a family. Kids today seem to think they need a year or five in between each of those steps, and before you know it, you're married, sure, but you're pushing forty and just starting to think about a family. Don't do that to yourself." Amos' hands dropped to the bed, his left arm and hand quivering.

Malachi nodded. Marriage. The thought didn't scare him like it had yesterday. What had that panic been about? Was it simply because he'd been taken by surprise? She'd tended him last night, making soup, snuggling with him on the sofa. It had killed him to leave. He wanted that every night. He wanted to have a chance to tend her when she needed it.

"She didn't return the sentiment. But she didn't run screaming, either. So I guess we'll see what happens. Believe me, there'll be a lot of prayer. Anyway, I brought you a muffin, hungry?" He reached for the paper sack he'd dropped at Amos' feet.

"Oh yeah."

"How long will Mr. Greenway be in the hospital?" Ursula slipped her hand into Malachi's.

He wove his fingers through hers and gave them a light squeeze. "Three to six days, depending. I think his daughter said they were leaning toward four. So two more after today? But she—the daughter—wants him to move to Retro Village. He doesn't want to give up the house."

Ursula winced. "That's...hard. She didn't offer for him to go live with her?"

"Don't know. Maybe she did, but I can't see Amos giving up on Arcadia Valley. He's lived here almost his whole life. In that house. If he doesn't want to leave the house, why would he willingly leave the town?"

"To live with people who love him and want to help, maybe?"

Malachi smiled. That was a point. Not one Amos was likely open to hearing though. The stroke had caused only minimal damage, which was a blessing. The doctors figured that Malachi had showed up fairly soon afterward, so the brain damage had been limited. But Amos still had a long road ahead of him. Right now, he could sign— basically—with both hands, but his left leg was useless. And if he couldn't get around on his own, then the retirement center where nurses were available at all hours was the best choice. Well, second best. Going home with his daughter would be best, but... "He's pretty stubborn. I tried to stay out of it, which his daughter appreciated, though it made Amos angry."

"Stuck in the middle. Poor Mal." Ursula bumped his hip with hers as they walked through Founders Park.

"Why do I get the feeling that wasn't sincere?" He smiled. Maybe he didn't get sarcasm, but he was pretty sure that's what that had been.

"I'm serious. Mostly." She grinned and leaned up until their lips met.

Malachi stopped and pulled her into his arms. Maybe she'd intended it to be a light kiss, but that didn't mean he had to leave it that way.

She eased back. Her cheeks were flushed, her eyes sparkling. She opened her mouth and then closed it.

"What?"

"Nothing. Let's walk. I need to get back to work. I have two new clients—both CSBs. Do I have you to thank for that?"

He shrugged. "I've joined a few online groups for them and might have mentioned how great our site is. It does everything we need and, other than that one hiccup where you fired us as your clients, you're easy to work with."

"Hey. That wasn't..." Ursula shook her head. "Idiot."

"I might not have mentioned that part. Glad it got you some business. I plan to take a box of cookies and muffins by the bridal shop when I'm in Twin Falls for pickups later this afternoon. Thanks for the tip. Of course, maybe she'll be happier with the store bought ones. But it never hurts to say hi. You want to come?"

She raised her eyebrows. "Come? To Twin Falls?"

"Sure. Pick up doesn't last that long. You could bring a book. Or your laptop—I have a decent enough data plan I don't mind making a hotspot with my cell. We could run a mission while we wait."

"You're going to come back to OQ? Really?" Ursula squeezed his hand as they headed back down the sidewalk toward the bakery. "I'm so glad. I never meant to chase you away from that. Even if we hadn't worked things out...you have friends other than me online."

"None that matter nearly as much." He paused and pulled her close for another kiss. "I love you."

She smiled and kissed the tip of his nose. "I need to run if I'm going to go with you. What time will you head out?"

Malachi fought a frown. Did she just not feel the same as him? Sure, it was better that she not say she loved him if she didn't. But...if that was the case, should he— what? Give up? Move on? That wasn't an option. Not yet. He'd just keep saying it until she said something. One way or the other. *Please, God, don't let it be the other.* "Three thirty?"

She nodded. "See you then."

He sighed and watched her jog across the street and head home. It was nice that she'd sprung him from the cramped office for a lunchtime walk. He rubbed the space over his heart. He loved her. And he needed her to love him back.

The older woman who sat behind the writing desk near the door looked up as Malachi held it open for Ursula.

"Good afternoon. Ursula, wasn't it? You were here earlier this week with Ruth?"

Ursula nodded, her cheeks pinking prettily. "Yes. Hi, Barbara. This is my, um, this is Malachi Baxter."

Barbara's eyebrows rose and she extended her hand.

Malachi shook it. "It's nice to meet you. My brothers and I have a bakery in Arcadia Valley. It's a CSB—Community Supported Bakery—anyway, Ursula thought you might enjoy our cookies."

"Well, I never say no to cookies." Barbara looked at Ursula. "Were they that bad?"

"No. Not bad...just...everything else is upscale and classy in here. They were dissonant." Ursula shifted from one foot to the other. "I didn't mean..."

Barbara smiled and flipped open the box. "It's fine. I've often felt the same way. We used to have a consultant who baked cookies each week and brought them in. And then she ended up finding the love of her life, choosing an amazing dress, and eloping. But we had a little bit of a reputation for offering tea and cookies, so I felt like we needed to continue. My skills, however, don't run to baking. My, these look delicious. Would you join me?"

"Oh. No thank you." Malachi held up his hands. "I've had some today already. The oatmeal chocolate chip are a favorite, so I always sneak a few when my brother makes them. I put our card in there as well. Feel free to get in touch with any questions."

Barbara bit into the cookie and chewed. "Mmm. You deliver?"

He nodded. "Wednesdays we have a pick up location here in Twin Falls and I have a few deliveries that I do as well."

"Thank you. I'll...probably be in touch." Barbara set the box down on the desk and crooked her finger at Ursula. "Before you go, could I show you some shoes I was thinking of for your friend? It won't take long."

Ursula glanced at Malachi.

He shrugged.

"Okay. Sure." Ursula followed behind Barbara.

Malachi watched them turn the corner before shifting his attention to the store. It was sparkly. And feminine. He couldn't quite picture his sister enjoying being there. Not that she wasn't feminine, but she wasn't girly. And this place reeked of girly. Still, maybe every woman wanted that on her wedding day. How was he supposed to know? His general feeling about weddings circled somewhere right around just tell him when to show up and where to stand. Not that he'd given weddings much thought in his lifetime. Had Ursula? Probably. All little girls did, right?

Several minutes later, Ursula came back with Barbara in her wake. "Thanks again."

Barbara nodded and extended her hand to Malachi. "It really was a pleasure meeting you. I'm sure I'll be in touch about the cookies."

Back in the car, Malachi shifted so he could see Ursula better. "What was that?"

"What? The shoes? They were shoes." She wouldn't quite meet his gaze. "But I'm guessing your sister already knows what she wants. And I also doubt she wants to spend two hundred dollars on a pair of shoes."

"For real? They're shoes. Do they walk for you?"

Ursula smiled and shook her head. "I don't expect you to understand. I mostly don't myself. Anyway, thanks for inviting me along."

He studied her. "Dinner?"

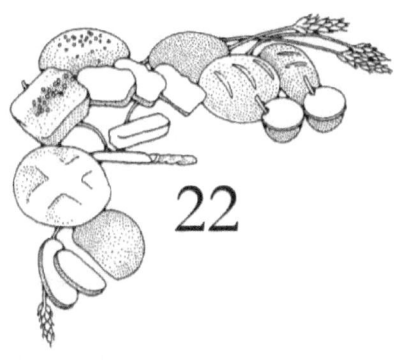

# 22

Ursula gave the potato salad another stir and licked the spoon before dropping it in the sink. It was good. Mixing in the Dijon—just a touch—really gave it a bit of a kick. Well, that and the hot sauce. But she never told anyone about that anymore. The one time she'd mentioned it, it had created entirely too much drama. What people didn't know couldn't hurt them. She covered the bowl with a sheet of foil and looked around. Was she forgetting something?

Triton meowed grumpily from beside his dish.

"I can't help that you ate it too fast. You don't get any more." She squatted and scratched his head until he started to purr. "That's better. Now you can have a pleasant day with the house all to yourself. I'm spending the day with Malachi and his family at their farm. Well, Corban's farm. I guess it's not theirs. But they're having a barbecue and Malachi invited me."

Triton cocked his head at her before butting her hand off and stalking away.

Ursula smiled. Cats kept you on your toes.

She and Malachi had seen each other for at least a few minutes every day since their Wednesday trip to Twin Falls. Every time they were together, he told her that he loved her. And still the words lodged in her throat. She cared for him. She wanted him in her life. Why couldn't she say the words back? She saw the hurt flash in his eyes when she didn't. Even though he'd never say anything about it.

She took a deep breath and let it out slowly. Today wasn't the day to worry about it. Today was for a Labor Day picnic with Malachi and his family. She was looking forward to seeing Ruth, too. The Fairview took up most of her time. They'd been particularly busy the last week with what came across, at least in texts, as high-maintenance guests. Hopefully Ruth could still get away and hang out with them. Ursula really didn't want to be the only woman there.

With the potato salad in hand, Ursula made her way to the car. She glanced over at Mr. Greenway's house. It was odd not seeing him out on the porch these days. Was he still in the hospital, or had he finally been released? Malachi would know. She made a mental note to ask as she settled the bowl in the foot space of the passenger seat. She pressed a hand to her stomach to quell the jitters and got in the car.

The drive to the farmhouse was short. A police car was parked on one side of the driveway. Ursula chuckled. Had they gotten that rowdy already? Who was around to hear? She parked next to the cop, not wanting to go behind and block it in.

Ruth grabbed the door handle of Ursula's car and dragged it open. "You made it. I was beginning to wonder."

She stepped out of the car and smoothed the skirt of the robin's egg blue sundress she'd decided on at the last minute. "Am I late?"

"No. Of course not. I've just been waiting for you." Ruth glanced across the lawn to where several people congregated around a big silver grill. "I'm not the only one."

"Yeah?" She took a deep breath and followed Ruth's look. "I'm kind of excited to see him, too."

"Here he comes. What did you bring? Just give it to me, I'll take it over to the table we set up and give you two some privacy." Ruth winked and circled the car. She opened the passenger door and grabbed the bowl before disappearing.

Malachi strolled over, his hands tucked in his pockets. "Hi."

"Hi yourself." Ursula turned to take in the setup. "This is more than just your family."

He nodded. "Corban invited some friends— Emerson and Pam and their two kids—as well as some folks from church. Word got out and...well, it turned into a bit of a party."

"Someone called the cops?"

He laughed. "No. That's Jonah's friend, Gloria. She comes by the bakery just about every day. I think he's smitten."

"Yeah? Oh, she's who came to Mr. Greenway's." She didn't know Jonah super well, but he seemed nice enough. Plus he was the mastermind behind most of the baking, which was its own recommendation. "Do you know if Mr. Greenway is out of the hospital yet? Every time I look at his house and don't see him out on the porch, I get sad."

"Tomorrow. But...he's not going home. His daughter is strong-arming him into Retro Village. Turns out, moving in with her wasn't given as an option—I guess her husband isn't on board with it—so it's Retro Village or a nursing facility near her. I get the impression that she doesn't visit very often, didn't even when she and her husband lived here in town, so living close doesn't hold as much appeal as staying in Arcadia Valley. Selfishly I'm glad." Malachi took her hand and tugged her to his side. "Did I mention you look lovely? Because you do."

Her insides went gooey. She tipped her head up and brushed her lips over his. "Thanks."

"Come on, I'll introduce you to everyone. Or at least everyone I know. I'm not sure I have all the names straight. Then we can eat. The ribs should be done soon." He drew her with him toward the small crowd on the lawn.

There were picnic tables and blankets spread out in a haphazard array. A long table along the porch was loaded with bowls, platters, and bottles. A tub sat on the ground at one end, cans and bottles poking up out of ice. Conversation floated around on the breeze. It sounded like the end of summer barbecue it was.

Jonah manned the grill. A woman in uniform stood nearby, chatting with him as he poked at ribs and flipped over burgers.

Malachi stopped by Jonah and touched his arm before signing quickly.

Jonah grinned and turned. "Hey, Ursula. Glad you could make it. Have you met Gloria?"

"Briefly, sort of. But not under such pleasant circumstances." Ursula extended her hand.

Gloria smiled and took it. "I hear you're responsible for the bakery website?"

She nodded.

"You did a great job. Still taking new business or do you have enough to stay busy?"

"I can always use a new client." Ursula flipped open the clasp of her small purse and dragged out the silver card case she'd thrown in at the last minute.

Gloria took the card. "Thanks. I can't promise anything, but I have a friend who's a potter. She does most of her business online and her website...stinks. I've told her, and she admits it, but she's been determined to do it all herself. And, well, websites aren't her strong suit. But her pottery is amazing and deserves better."

"Cool. I love working art and e-commerce into a site, so I hope she gets in touch." Ursula's back warmed where Malachi placed his hand. "It was nice to meet you."

Malachi steered her to another group of people. This time he tapped Corban on the arm and signed more slowly.

Corban made introductions and Ursula tried to keep up as he rattled off names. She managed a few words with everyone before Malachi led her to another group. This time it was Micah who did the talking. And she officially lost track of who was who and what kids went with which parents. Maybe it'd all come together at some point, but for now, she fell back on smiling and nodding.

"Ready to eat?" Malachi nudged her with his elbow.

"I am. This is nice. You've plugged in so quickly to the town. I'm a little jealous."

He shook his head. "Not me. It's all Ruth and Corban. Jonah and Micah to a lesser degree. I just get brought along for the ride."

They approached the table at the same time as Jonah brought a heaping plate of ribs over from the grill. He grinned and cupped his hands around his mouth. "Can I get everyone's attention?"

Gradually the conversation died down. Jonah nodded. "Thanks so much for coming out to relax and celebrate the end of summer with us. The food's all ready—and it looks amazing. So before we all dig in, why don't we get Corban to say the blessing?"

Corban jolted and then, with red creeping up his neck, he tugged the ball cap he was wearing off his head and cleared his throat. "Let's pray. Heavenly Father, thank you for this beautiful day, the sunshine, the food, and the friendship that we have here. Help us to glorify you in all we do. Please bless this food to our bodies, and our bodies to your service. Amen."

Mutters of amen echoed around the small crowd.

Ursula blinked away the tears that tried to form. This was what she'd been missing. And she hadn't even realized it.

Malachi handed her a plate before taking one for himself. "You okay?"

She nodded and kissed his cheek. "Just really happy to be here."

The afternoon was filled with laughter and food. Lots and lots of food. People came and went as their schedules allowed—there were other gatherings to attend and last days at neighborhood swimming pools to take advantage of, after all. Ursula drifted between clumps of people, usually with Malachi at her side, though he disappeared here and there as well when one of his siblings needed him.

"Having fun?" Ruth slipped up behind her as she watched several kids playing a cutthroat game of tag.

"I am."

Ruth laughed. "Don't sound so surprised."

Ursula hunched her shoulders. "Sorry. But I didn't expect to. I was looking forward to seeing Malachi—and you—but didn't expect to stay as long as I have."

"Well, before you run off, I really want to show you something. Come walk with me?"

Ursula pushed herself out of the chair she'd snagged when Malachi had darted inside with a promise to be back quickly. He'd been gone five minutes. Would he think she left? "Do you know where your brother is?"

"Mal? He's helping Jonah with the ice cream maker. I told him I was going to grab you. He won't think you've run off."

"I'm that easy to read?"

Ruth shook her head. "No. But I'm in love myself, so I know how the brain works. Come on."

Ursula's jaw dropped just the tiniest bit. She wasn't—but Ruth was already striding around the back of the house. She hurried to catch up with her friend. "Why would you say that?"

"Hmm?" Ruth looked over at her, curiosity written on her features. "Say what?"

"About me being in love?"

With a small chuckle, Ruth opened the gate set in a white picket fence. "Aren't you?"

Ursula sighed. She didn't *know*. And that was the problem. Her mother's advice was hard to wrap her mind around. Could she just choose to be in love? There had to be more than that. "I don't know."

"Ah." Ruth patted her arm. "Well, you'll figure it out. Isn't this lovely?"

Ursula pulled her thoughts back and looked around at the garden. The roses were clinging to their last blooms and the waterfall in the corner bubbled merrily. The rest of the plants had, by and large, passed their prime. But they were still beautiful. "It is. What is it?"

"It was Corban's mother's garden. She, apparently, wanted to grow something other than vegetables and wheat. And she'd come and sit out here in the evenings with Corban's dad." Ruth moved to the bench by the water feature and sat, patting the space next to her. "I sneak over sometimes, when the B&B gets overwhelming or if I'm homesick for D.C. Corban proposed right here."

Ursula smiled. It was a good location, all things considered. The cheerful fall of water, the plants—in the spring the flowers must have been a riot of color. "I suspect I'd do the same. Do you really get homesick?"

Ruth shrugged. "Not as much anymore. It was time to leave—and with my brothers here and having found Corban...my whole life is here. But moving, even when you're ready to go, is hard. Why don't you think you're in love with Mal? Is it okay if I ask?"

"I guess." Ursula cleared her throat and tried to assemble her thoughts into something that would make sense. This was, after all, exactly what girlfriends were for. And maybe as someone newly in love, Ruth would have a better explanation than her mom. "It's largely because I've never been in love before. The guys I dated in high school were mostly friends. And maybe there were a few tingles when we kissed, but I also knew that they weren't going to be someone I married, so I never let myself get too wrapped up in them."

"Not a member of the 'every date is a potential mate' club?" Ruth laughed.

"Ugh. No. Though my youth pastor was big on that. And I understand the theory—now that I'm older it makes sense. But in high school...it was just dorky."

"Does that mean you consider Malachi a potential mate?"

Back to her brother. Which was good. She nodded. "I care for him. A lot."

"But you don't see him as a necessary part of your future?"

Did she? Ursula tried to imagine the years ahead. Malachi was always there. How much of that was because he was here, now, though? "I can't really picture the future without him."

Ruth nodded. "Which leads me back to my initial observation. You love him. It's scary to admit, I get that. But I know my brother about as well as anyone, I think. So I'm just going to say one more thing and let it go. Don't leave him hanging for too long. He can be patient, but not forever, and it hurts him that you're not willing to take that next step."

Willing. She was willing, wasn't she? "I'm not unwilling...I'm just not sure how."

Someone hollered for Ruth and she stood. "You just make a choice. It's both that simple and that difficult. I think that's Corban—you can sit here a while if you want."

Ursula nodded and watched the water trickle over rocks as Ruth scurried off. Back to a choice. Was it one she'd already made but wasn't willing to admit? She spent her time focusing on when she would see him again whenever they were apart. And when they were together, she never wanted it to end. It was easy to picture a life with him. Maybe it wasn't as mysterious as she was making it.

She looked over when Malachi sat beside her.

He smiled and brushed his fingers across her cheek. "Ruth said you might still be here. There's ice cream. You want to go get some?"

Ursula leaned in and pressed her lips to his.

When she eased back, he wiggled his eyebrows. "I should tell you about ice cream more often."

She chuckled. "I do love ice cream. But I love you more."

A slow grin spread across his face, and his eyes lit up. Malachi drew her closer and gently brought their lips together again. Maybe the ice cream could wait.

How was it already nearing the end of September? The past two weeks had flown by with website work that continued to pour in thanks to Malachi's CSB groups. She and Mal spent nearly every evening together as well. He'd gotten in the habit of swinging by with a box of two muffins on his way home from the bakery and staying for supper. Sometimes he'd bring his laptop and they'd sit together on the couch and play Orion's Quest. It was a subtly different dynamic having him right beside her and also online. But the change was a good one. Most evenings they ended with a walk in the moonlight. Now she understood a little more why her parents took their after-dinner strolls.

Tonight, rather than their usual Friday night game extravaganza, Malachi had made reservations at L'Aubergine. She'd never been. It didn't seem like the place you went by yourself. Not that Ursula was the kind of person who'd sit in a restaurant alone anyway. Before Malachi, she was the take-out queen. Ordering to go and sitting at home with Triton was better than sitting at a table and imagining everyone laughing at her because she was dining solo. Except...the thought of dining out alone wasn't quite so bizarre now. She scoffed. Now that it was unlikely to be an issue.

Ursula took a dress out of her closet and held it up in front of her. It was the nicest piece of clothing she owned, and she blessed her mother for insisting she buy it last Christmas when she'd been home. Navy blue with white piping on the three-quarter sleeves and around the scooped neck, the dress had an asymmetrical peplum that added just the right touch of interest at the waist. It wasn't vintage, but she could see the influences. And it looked great. Definitely L'Aubergine worthy.

"What do you think, Triton?" She spun, showing off the dress to the cat who lounged on her bed. He licked his paw and groomed his ears. Well. No accounting for feline taste. "Do you think he'll propose?"

Triton flicked an ear and turned to bathing his rear legs. Ursula chuckled and scrubbed his head. She and Malachi had talked more and more about marriage when they got together, the conversations shifting from generic thoughts to specific pictures of what a life built by the two of them would be. She shivered. When Malachi mentioned going to the fanciest place in town...well, what else could it be? She wasn't getting her hopes up—at least she was trying not to.

The knock on the door jolted her out of her thoughts. She gave Triton a final rub as she slid her feet into the heeled sandals that she'd bought the same day as the dress and hurried to the door. Malachi wore a suit. She had to stop and swallow as her heart took off like someone had fired the starting pistol at a race. "Wow."

He ran a hand down his tie and smiled, his eyes glinting appreciatively. "I could say the same. You're beautiful. And I'm sorry it's taken me this long to plan a fancy date. Ready?"

Ursula nodded. She pulled the door closed behind her and checked that it was locked then stopped and slipped her arm through his. Her gaze landed on the For Sale sign in Mr. Greenway's lawn and she sighed. She touched Malachi's arm and pointed across the street. "Did you see that?"

"I knew it was coming. I've been trying to visit Amos every few days. He's settling in, I guess. His daughter saw that he got moved over and then went home. I think she was only in town a week. He's feeling abandoned worse than when Alma died."

"That's terrible. Do you think he'd mind if I visited?"

Malachi shook his head and pulled open the car door. "He'd love it."

Ursula reached for the seatbelt as Malachi shut the door and circled the car. Would he? She'd never really spoken to the man. They'd exchanged waves. That was it. All her best intentions to visit him in the hospital had never come about—she'd meant to ask to go along with Malachi so he could introduce her. "Maybe I could go with you the next time you go?"

"Sure. Do you like puzzles?"

"What kind?"

"The kind you put together on a table. What other kind are there?"

She grinned. So many kinds—word puzzles, number puzzles—heck, Sudoku was basically a puzzle, wasn't it? "Sure, they're okay. Why?"

"Amos spends a good bit of time working on puzzles with a few of the other residents in the Frank Sinatra pod over at the village. He always invites me to join them." Malachi started the car and backed out of her driveway.

Ursula looked out the window. It wasn't far to the restaurant—not much was far when you were talking about a town the size of Arcadia Valley—but her feet, at least, were grateful they'd driven. Her shoes were already pinching.

At the restaurant, they were seated in the front room, near the large picture window that looked out over the sleepy town. There were several other diners—even one woman eating alone. Ursula shook her head. That woman had more self-confidence than she'd probably ever manage to drum up. Good for her.

The menu, in its thick leather cover, set her mouth watering. So many options. She'd have to make a point of coming back and trying something new—her gaze darted to Malachi as he pored over the offerings—he'd be up for that, wouldn't he? She made up her mind and closed the folder. Malachi did the same.

"What did you decide on?"

"The oregano chicken. You?" It briefly registered that he signed more than spoke these days. Ursula responded in kind. She enjoyed signing—it was like they had their own private language. She'd always been fascinated by couples who spoke something other than English to one another and wondered what it would be like to have that level of privacy. Now she had that, too. It was fun.

"I thought the porchetta sounded good."

Ursula frowned and reached for her menu. She hadn't seen that.

He reached across the table and tapped the specials. Ah. She wrinkled her nose. "You like Brussels sprouts?"

He grinned. "Sure. Don't you?"

"Yuk. No." She set the menu aside. "I'll stick with the chicken and the very sensible potatoes that come with it."

He laughed and reached across the table for her hand.

Malachi offered her his hand as she got out of the car. Moonlight streamed down from the clear skies above.

Dinner had been wonderful. They'd lingered over their meal and shared a dessert...and no proposal had been forthcoming. Ursula fought to keep her spirits up. She'd built up some ridiculous expectation—well, maybe not ridiculous. After all, they'd been talking about it more and more. It wasn't unreasonable to think that a fancy dinner out...she fought a sigh. Malachi was probably too traditional to propose so soon. They'd only really known each other since July. Even though they'd been friends online for more than two years. Maybe he didn't count that time?

She smiled and squeezed his fingers. "I had a lovely time."

"Me too. But then, I always do when I'm with you."

Ursula dug in her purse for her key.

Malachi lifted her chin and held her gaze. "I love you."

Her breath caught. Was this it? "I love you."

He kissed her then took the key from her limp fingers and unlocked the door for her with a twinkle in his eye. "Good night."

"Yeah. Good night." She blinked back tears and managed a tight smile before hurrying inside and closing the door. She turned the lock and headed toward her bedroom. A quick glance over her shoulder showed Malachi leaving the porch with his hands in his pockets. She hurried to her room and let the tears fall. Triton crawled up her arm and butted her cheek with his head.

The hot ball lodged in her chest wouldn't ease. Ursula gathered the cat in her arms and sobbed.

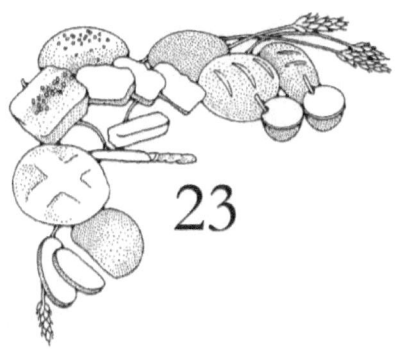

## 23

Malachi strolled into the common area of Retro Village's Frank Sinatra pod. Amos sat in his usual spot at one of the tables working a puzzle. Another puzzle, partially completed, took up a nearby table. He pulled out a chair and sat before pointing to the other puzzle and signing, "Why aren't you working on that one?"

"That's Clarence's. He's nice enough, but I try not to work on it when he's not around to help. They've got a million of these things." Amos shrugged.

Malachi pursed his lips. It was obvious his friend still hadn't really adjusted to being here. How long would it take? Or, when you were more than ninety years old, did you just not have to adjust if you didn't want to? "Feel like a walk?"

"Might as well. At least keep the nurses off my case. They nag all day long about how I have to practice if I'm going to regain my strength. But what's the point? I'm stuck here now, aren't I? It's not like if I get back on my feet all the way they'll let me go home. Don't got a home to go back to anyway, now." Amos frowned, but he wobbled to his feet and reached for the walker that stood nearby.

"I'm sorry, Amos." Malachi stood and watched the old man wrestle with the walker before shuffling forward a step. "There's a garden out this way. Want to look around?"

Amos nodded and pointed his walker toward the hall. It wasn't far, but it still broke Malachi's heart to see his friend looking his age. He'd been so vibrant and full of life before the stroke and now...he'd given up.

Out in the garden, a few more residents were taking advantage of the warm, sunlit Saturday. They were nearing the end of September, which meant the days like this were going to disappear. Fall, and then winter, were on their way. Corban had talked a lot about the final vegetable harvest and putting in the winter wheat this past week. In D.C., Malachi had only noticed the seasons from a "what to wear" standpoint. Living in Arcadia Valley he'd started to tune in to some of the rhythm of a life lived closer to the land. It was...interesting.

They made a circuit of the short path before Amos angled toward a bench that sat in the sunshine. He sat and gave his walker an annoyed look. "Can't talk when I'm walking now. Need my hands for both. And I know I sound like a peevish old man. Can't seem to stop myself."

Malachi grinned. "You have good reason. Change is hard, no matter the age. I've been praying for you—I'll keep doing it. I have to believe it'll get easier. And you're making some friends, right?"

"I guess. I miss my house. All my memories of Alma were there. Now they're stuck in my head and some days that makes them harder to reach." Amos made a frustrated gesture. "Never mind me. How are you? How's your girl?"

"I took her to L'Aubergine last night. That was a good call. She seemed to enjoy getting dressed up, though I could've done without having to wear a tie."

Amos shook his head. "It's good for you. I used to wear a tie every Sunday—sign of respect. Young people these days don't get it. Food was good?"

"Very. But...she got quiet, withdrawn at the end. And I got the feeling she was upset about something. And I have no idea what."

"Women." Amos winked. "Take me through the evening and maybe this old man can come up with an idea."

Malachi did. Walking through the night didn't help him any more than the million times he'd done it during his sleepless night. Maybe Amos' outside eyes would see something obvious.

"Hmm." Amos drummed his fingers on his knee. "You've been talking about marriage, you said?"

Malachi nodded.

The old man grinned. His shoulders began to shake, then bent forward like he was coughing.

"Are you okay?" Malachi searched the area for a nurse. Should he leave and get help?

Amos waved his hands in front of his face and wiped his eyes. "Laughing, boy. Just laughing. I think I know the problem."

"And it's funny?"

"When you're as old as I am it is." Amos patted Malachi's knee. "You ever taken her somewhere fancy before?"

Malachi shook his head. "We stay in a lot and talk, or play our computer game. We go for walks. That kind of thing. Why?"

"I suspect she thought you were planning to propose. Bit of a letdown when you didn't, don't you think?"

"Oh." Malachi closed his eyes and called up the couple of times Ursula had braced herself throughout the evening. He was an idiot. "You might just be right. Now what do I do?"

"Depends, I guess, on whether you're ready to take that leap."

Was he? They'd only known each other since July. Well...that wasn't completely true. He'd been in love with her for nearly two years before they ever met in person. Before he knew her name. But she hadn't felt that way about him. She'd considered him her online friend, sure, but that was the end of it. Loving him was a recent development. Wouldn't he be pushing her if he bought her a ring now? "Ultimately. It just seemed too soon."

"Son. If she's disappointed that you didn't ask, she's going to say yes when you do."

Malachi parked the car at the curb in front of Amos' house and looked across the street at Ursula's. Lights glowed from the windows and he could just make out the shadow of Triton in his usual spot. She was expecting him. He'd called and asked if he could bring dinner over after he badgered Jonah into putting together something special just for them. It hadn't taken as much persuasion as he'd figured it would. Neither had talking Ruth into a quick trip to Facets, the local jewelry store. In fact, his sister had practically bounced the whole way there. But she'd been more helpful than he'd imagined, and not only because the clerk had been a mumbler. He never would've been able to read the man's lips well enough to make sure he knew exactly what he was getting.

Ruth had dragged Ursula out in the afternoon, as well, going down to Twin Falls to look at the shoes. No one was more surprised than he was when she actually bought them. But it had given him a window when he'd known Ursula wouldn't be online so he could contact her dad. That had been...awkward. There was no other word for it. But he couldn't ask her to marry him without at least trying to talk to her parents first. And, after having said yes, Ursula's dad also mentioned that this was the first time his wife had been willing to sit with him while he was logged into the game. So there was that.

And he was stalling. He took a deep breath and pushed open the door, then grabbed the insulated carrier from the back seat. They'd eat first and then...he wanted to ask her out on her tiny little deck, with the moonlight shining in her eyes.

She opened the door before he could knock and smiled. It didn't quite reach her eyes though. "I wondered if you were going to come in, or if you were just going to sit in your car and watch the house."

"Sorry." He lifted the bag of food. "Hungry?"

"Sure."

Malachi followed her into the kitchen. She was upset with him. And...sad. He set the food down and crossed to where she was lifting plates down from the cupboard and took her into his arms.

Ursula relaxed against him, her head dropping to his shoulder.

He pressed a kiss to her forehead and took the plates. "Jonah cooked one of the specials from the restaurant he used to work at for us. I haven't had it before, but it smells great."

"That was nice of him. What can I do to help?"

"Just sit. It's all ready." Malachi reached in the bag and took out containers, transferring the contents to their plates. He set one in front of Ursula and the other at his spot.

"It smells good. What is it?" Ursula leaned closer and inhaled.

"Chicken scaloppini with angel hair and asparagus. And extra capers, because he knows I love them. You can pick them off if you want to." Malachi pushed a little basket of bread into the center of the table. "And garlic bread. He said you can't do without that."

This time her smile was genuine. "It's hard to say no to, that's for sure."

Malachi reached for her hand and held it until she met his gaze. "I love you, Ursula."

"I love you, too."

Hmm. She still seemed upset. Maybe he should have asked first...but he really wanted to wait until the sun had set. He said a quick blessing over their meal and they dug in.

Ursula talked about her shoe-shopping trip with Ruth. His sister had tried on nine different pairs of wedding shoes—and honestly, who knew there were such things as wedding shoes?

"Why can't you just wear regular white shoes?"

Ursula laughed. "This was my question. But apparently even her feet need to sparkle when she marries Corban. They're lovely shoes, I'll give her that. Still. Whatever makes her happy, I guess."

"I think that's Corban. The rest is just icing." Malachi scraped the last bite up from his plate. He was excessively aware of the ring box in his pocket. Would she like it? Maybe it was time to find out. "Let's go out on the deck."

Ursula shrugged. "Okay. Did you want dessert? I have some—"

"I brought something. I just thought maybe we could wait a little, let everything settle."

She nodded and took his offered hand.

Malachi focused on his breathing as his heart began to race. He pulled open the door to the small deck and stepped out into the light of the rising moon. Perfect.

Ursula rubbed her arms. "Chillier than I expected."

Was it? He turned and pulled her close. "Better?"

She nodded.

He swallowed. Everything he'd planned to say evaporated. Malachi took a step away and turned to face her. He signed while he spoke, his gaze locked with hers. "I love you. Maybe you don't know I've loved you for close to two years now. Even though I only knew you online, I knew you were the woman I wanted to spend my life with. I just thought it was a pipe dream. And then I met you, and I can't imagine not having you with me."

Ursula blinked, her eyes shining.

Malachi took the ring box out of his pocket and lowered to one knee before opening it and offering it to her. "Marry me, Ursula, please? I need you in my life for always."

With shaking hands, Ursula reached for the ring. A tear slipped down her cheek and she laughed and brushed it away. "Of course I'll marry you. I love you, Malachi Baxter."

He stood and helped her ease the ring onto her finger. She held it out so it could sparkle in the moonbeams.

Malachi pulled her close and lowered his lips to hers. There'd be time for muffins—and moonbeams—later. They had forever.

# Arcadia Valley Romance:
# Six authors. Six series. One community.

Welcome to Arcadia Valley, Idaho, where a foodie culture and romance grow hand-in-hand. Join my friends and me as we release a book every month set in Arcadia Valley. You'll enjoy meeting old friends and making new ones as each of the six authors' books intertwine with the previous stories in this Christian romance series. Get started with Romance Grows in Arcadia Valley and follow along at ArcadiaValleyRomance.com to make sure you don't miss any installments!

AN
## Arcadia Valley
### ROMANCE

www.ArcadiaValleyRomance.com

Javier Quintana knows his family's struggling restaurant, El Corazon, needs help. But when his interfering siblings hire Molly Abbott, a successful food entrepreneur and his high-school sweetheart, he's livid. The way their relationship ended wasn't pretty. And although Molly never married, she's the single mom of a twelve-year-old daughter conceived right about the time of the breakup.

Molly's ideas about farm-to-table, health-conscious Mexican food conflict with Javier's strong sense of tradition, even as her joyous faith convicts him about his own lapse from the church of his youth. Can a reunion romance bring happiness to two lonely souls who never forgot each other... or will their relationship be derailed by the secrets they both carry in their hearts?

Javier Quintana raked his fingers through his hair and tried to concentrate on the laptop computer in front of him and the stack of bills beside him. The empty dining room of El Corazon provided no distraction. Sure, they were closed on Mondays, but the trouble was that the place was all too empty at dinnertime the rest of the week.

The restaurant wasn't going under...at least not yet. But it was definitely in the red.

He looked up at the portrait of his mother and father on the wall. They'd started the restaurant as newlyweds. All four of the kids had grown up there, hanging around, helping, doing homework at this very table, moving back into the kitchen when the dinner rush started.

Now, there wasn't much of a dinner rush.

He'd promised his father, and then his mother, to keep the restaurant in the family, to keep it going.

The cold, dry bills and papers around him seemed to crush the colorful, happy place his parents had made.

Behind him, the restaurant's front door opened.

"We're closed," he called without looking up.

"Hello?" The voice sounded like... No, it couldn't be. He straightened his shirt as he strode through the entryway to the door.

And froze.

Molly?

In a flash he was eighteen again, in love with his whole young heart.

He blinked and refocused his eyes. Yes, Molly Abbot stood there, framed by the golden light of a late-August day.

His heart stopped, stuttered, and then settled into pounding, hard and fast.

She was even more beautiful than she'd been in high school. Big eyes, cornsilk blonde hair full around her shoulders. She was still a tiny little thing, dressed professionally now, but with the big, dangly earrings she'd always favored.

Yes, it was the same Molly he'd loved. The same Molly who'd betrayed him.

Anger drew him up to his full six-two, and it was only his wired-in manners that prevented him from slamming the door in her face, shutting out the beauty and the pain.

"Hey, Javier, it's definitely been awhile." She seemed to be looking past him into the restaurant.

He crossed his arms and clenched his jaw.

"I was supposed to meet you guys here... Veronica said you knew all about it. Maybe I'm a little early?" She checked her watch. "I can come back when everyone's here. I don't want to be a way from my daughter too long--"

What meeting was she talking about? And how could she have the audacity to talk to him about her daughter?

He tried to school his face, to focus on the chirping birds and crickets, the hot air pushing its way through the open door behind her and into the restaurant's air-conditioned coolness. From the parking lot, the sweet aroma of pineapple weed blew in.

"Or, maybe this is a blessing." Her hand came up to twist her hair, which had always been her tell for anxiety. "Maybe we can talk a little."

He still hadn't said one word to her and she seemed to realize that, finally. She looked down at the ground, or maybe she was just checking out the way the parking lot's dust had taken the shine off her designer shoes.

"Can I come in?"

No.

No way.

He stepped back to let her pass. Why was she here? Why, after all this time, and acting like she belonged here?

She walked in and did a turn around the dining room, totally calm. Analytical, almost. "The place still looks the same."

All the love and all the pain he'd felt about her surged up at her words, covered over with a glaze of terrible, terrible hurt.

This was nothing to her. She felt nothing.

He swallowed down his emotions, trying to make way for some civilized words to pass, but he couldn't quite get there. "Don't try to make small talk." He knew his voice was harsh. "You're not welcome."

She looked at him full on then, met his eyes with her blue ones, and he realized: she's not ashamed; she's surprised. And maybe a little angry.

Car doors slammed in the parking lot, and a few seconds later his brothers and sister pushed into the restaurant. "Hey, Javier! We're here!"

"Molly beat us!" Veronica reached out and hugged Molly, which felt to Javier like a betrayal. "Hey, girl, how are you?"

"Sorry we're late, we would've been on time if it weren't for lover boy here." Daniel punched Alex in the arm.

Alex held his hands up like stop signs. "Hey, I had to help my girl move into her new apartment. What else does a fiancé do?" He seemed to be trying to keep a silly grin off his face, but it wasn't working.

A slight feeling of satisfaction pushed past Javier's distress. It was good to see Alex so happy. One of his siblings had found a good woman, at least.

They'd come to a stop in a semicircle around him, all quieting down a little. Javier was the oldest brother, and since Papa had died, he'd been the head of the family. They treated him with respect rather than the clowning around they did with each other. But right now, his brothers and his sister had identical guilty looks in their eyes.

He couldn't bear to look at Molly, to try to dissect whatever she might be feeling.

He cleared his throat. "What memo did I miss?"

Veronica stepped forward and put an arm around him, leaning her head against his shoulder. "We're kind of doing an intervention."

"We know how hard you've been working," Alex began, then broke off. Despite having been a big deal major league baseball player, he tended to defer to his older brothers.

"And we know the restaurant isn't doing real well." Daniel perched on the edge of a table, looking around the room. Whatever they were up to must be serious, to get Daniel to actually come to the restaurant in the first place, and to leave his twins behind in the second place, dedicated single dad that he was.

"And once I start school and this new job, I'm going to be even less help," Alex said.

"And I have no life as it is, what with the girls and my practice. You already know I'm no help." Daniel twisted his head from side to side and pushed clasped hands out in front of him, stretching his neck. Chiropracting on himself.

"And even though I'm here every day, I can't figure out how to fix whatever's wrong with El Corazon," Veronica said. "Plus, you turned down the other two consultants we brought in…"

It was true; he had. They'd been idiots. "Get to the point," he ordered his siblings.

"We kind of decided something on our own," Veronica said.

"Took it to a vote," Alex said, "and all three of us agreed, so… " He trailed off.

"We went ahead and hired Molly." Daniel said, his voice firm. He put an arm around Molly's shoulders.

A flush of angry heat rose in Javier's face and neck, whether because of the idea that they'd hired her, or because of Daniel touching her, he couldn't say for sure.

"She's a food entrepreneur," Veronica explained, "who knows all about the fresh-food movement."

"She turned around three restaurants in Cleveland."

"And one of them's a traditional Mexican place."

"And she knows El Corazon, because she practically spent high school here."

Which was exactly the problem. She'd humiliated him in front of the entire town.

She shrugged out from under Daniel's arm and held up a slender, delicate hand, looking from Javier to Veronica, Daniel, and Alex. "Hold up. I thought Javier knew about this and agreed to it."

His siblings all started to talk, but she put a hand on her hip and shook her head. "From the preliminary research I've done, he's the main manager and the rest of you are only peripherally involved, Daniel not at all." She frowned severely at them. "And you sprung this on him?"

"You know how he is, Mol." Alex lifted his hands, palms up.

"Stubborn and bull-headed," Veronica added.

He was watching her—he couldn't help it—so he saw the emotion that flashed across her face. She did know how he was.

Something else flashed: the small silver cross around her neck, the same one she'd worn back when he'd known her in high school. He remembered touching it when he'd kissed her. It had reminded him of her purity and kept him from going too far.

She hadn't held to the same rules with the next guy, obviously.

"I want her out of here."

She raised her eyebrows and looked at him steadily for a few seconds, then looked around at his siblings. "So I'm going to go back to Uncle Dale's house and help my daughter get ready for the first day of school." She paused, then spoke again. "We do have a back-out clause in the contract, but I hope it won't come to that since I've pulled up stakes and moved." She gave Javier a cool glance. And then, her back straight, she stalked out of the restaurant.

Immediately, his brothers and sister started talking.

"That was so rude!" Veronica slapped his arm.

"No way to talk to a lady," Alex scolded.

"We can't afford her back-out clause." That was Daniel, his worry lines—perpetual with him since the loss of his wife—deepening in his face. "If we don't hire her, I don't know what else we can do."

"Just because you never got over her..."

He held up a hand. "Stop."

"But—"

"I mean it. Stop."

They all shut their mouths, thankfully, though he knew that wouldn't last.

"I don't appreciate your doing this without consulting me. You know, just like everyone else in town, what happened between us twelve years ago. Why would you think we could work together?"

"But would you have hired her if you'd known?" Veronica asked.

"I'm telling you, she's the only person who can do this for us," Alex said. "She knows the green food culture, and she knows our traditions."

"You've been alone too long," Daniel said. "You don't trust women."

"You should talk," Veronica said, elbowing Daniel.

"I don't trust her," Javier said flatly.

"See, this is all part of your personality issues." Veronica pushed herself into the curve of his arm. As the little sister, she could get away with saying things their brothers couldn't, and she knew it. "You have to do everything yourself, you're over-responsible, you're controlling. This time, that's not working."

"Look," Alex said, "we all have the best interests of El Corazon at heart. We hate to see it go under. But when you were in Mexico and I was running the place, I saw the truth. That's where we're heading."

"And I'm just not ready for that." Veronica's voice sounded shaky. "I'm not ready to lose this world I grew up in. The world Mama and Papa made." She glanced over at the framed photograph of their parents.

Javier looked at the photograph too, and then stared down at the tile floor. As the oldest brother, it was his job to care for them. Right now, he was more of an impediment to getting things done, at least from the way they were describing it.

Not only that, he was outnumbered. They all four had a quarter interest in the restaurant, and if three of them had made a decision, he should—had to, really—go along with it.

But work with Molly Abbot? The woman who'd played him for a fool and broken his heart?

"I'll think about it," he growled just to get them out of his hair. "Now, everybody needs to leave. I've got work to do."

# Books in the Arcadia Valley Romance Series

Want a Free Book?

If you enjoyed Muffins & Moonbeams and would like to read another of my full-length novels for free, you can get a free download of Courage to Change simply by signing up for my newsletter here: http://bit.ly/2g0AGvf

## Author's Note

Thank you for reading Muffins & Moonbeams! I hope that you enjoyed it! I would appreciate it if you'd help others enjoy it too by leaving a review! Word of mouth is how most people say they find new books to read, so I'd love it if you'd also consider telling your friends about it. Any success my books have is owed to readers like you who take the time to tell others about my stories. Thank you, from the bottom of my heart.

Working on this project, with the five other amazing authors who are all writing in Arcadia Valley, has been an absolute delight. I love all the characters who fill up our little town, and I hope you will, too. Each of the ladies who are a part of Arcadia Valley has a great talent and a deep love for Christian fiction. I think you'll agree it shows in the work they produce.

You can always keep up to date with my writing news via my newsletter. There's a sign-up form at my website http://bit.ly/2g0AGvf and also on my author Facebook page

http://www.Facebook.com/ElizabethMaddrey.

I continue to owe a huge debt of gratitude to my husband and sons for giving me the time to write, my sister for her unflinching support and encouragement, and my critique partners Lynellen Perry, Heather Gray and Jan Elder for catching all the times I use the same word six times in two paragraphs.

More than anything, I'm grateful that God continues to give me words and makes it possible for me to write them down.

I'd love to hear from you! You can connect with me on Facebook my webpage or via email.

## About the Author

Elizabeth Maddrey began writing stories as soon as she could form the letters properly and has never looked back. Though her practical nature and love of computers, math, and organization steered her into computer science at Wheaton College, she always had one or more stories in progress to occupy her free time. This continued through a Master's program in Software Engineering, several years in the computer industry, teaching programming at the college level, and a Ph.D. in Computer Technology in Education. When she isn't writing, Elizabeth is a voracious consumer of books and has mastered the art of reading while undertaking just about any other activity.

Elizabeth is the author of more than ten books, both fiction and non-fiction. She lives in the suburbs of Washington, D.C. with her husband and their two incredibly active little boys.